"Don't me, Martha."

Simon stepped toward her.

"If you think you're going to force anything out of me, Simon—" She stopped as he loomed over her.

"Force it out of you—no," he said almost gently. "But we might put something to the test."

"Simon," she whispered as he drew her into his arms, "that's not fair...."

"Isn't it? Don't you know what they say about love and war?"

LINDSAY ARMSTRONG was born in South Africa but now lives in Australia with her New Zealand-born husband and their five children. They have lived in nearly every state of Australia and tried their hand at some unusual, for them, occupations, such as farming and horse training— all grist to the mill for a writer! Lindsay started writing romance fiction when their youngest child began school and Lindsay was left feeling at a loose end. She is still doing it and loving it.

Books by Lindsay Armstrong

LINDSAY ARMSTRONG

Dangerous Deceiver

Harlequin Books

TORONTO • NEW YORK • LONDON
AMSTERDAM • PARIS • SYDNEY • HAMBURG
STOCKHOLM • ATHENS • TOKYO • MILAN
MADRID • WARSAW • BUDAPEST • AUCKLAND

ISBN 0-373-11874-0

DANGEROUS DECEIVER

First North American Publication 1997.

Copyright © 1995 by Lindsay Armstrong.

Printed in U.S.A.

CHAPTER ONE

'HE WAS——'

Martha Winters paused for two reasons: because she'd been about to describe Simon Macquarie as beautiful and because she was about to confide things she'd never told anyone before. But as she glanced at her friend Jane's woeful, tear-drenched face she sighed inwardly, and continued, although on a slightly different tack. 'He was extremely arrogant as a matter of fact. We didn't like each other much at all. Well...' She shrugged her slim shoulders and reflected that it was almost impossible to explain what had happened between her and Simon Macquarie, and that if Jane hadn't just been painfully ditched by her boyfriend she wouldn't even be trying to, in an effort to offer some consolation.

To make matters worse, Martha and Jane had shared a flat for two years and had become really close, but Martha was leaving for London in the morning and Jane, who was as tender-hearted as she was often gullible, was in a bad way about that as well.

'And he ditched you, Martha?' Fresh tears slid down Jane's face. 'You poor thing.'

Martha smiled slightly. 'It was three years ago, Jane. Do I look like a poor, abandoned thing?'

'No,' Jane replied consideringly. 'You always look wonderful and I know you'll be a sensation in London but I also happen to know there hasn't been a serious man in your life for the last two years, which is a bit incredible for a girl like you. Do you still love him or have you *sworn* never to be taken for a ride by any man again?' she asked dramatically.

Martha hesitated because despite stringent denials to herself over the years she still couldn't be sure that there mightn't be a grain of truth in both those propositions. So finally she said rather drily, 'If it was love it was also highly uncomfortable and the kind of love you're probably better off without; it was certainly one-sided and yes, you're right, I've been a bit wary ever since. But that's not to say,' she added briskly, 'that I've lost *all* faith in the right man coming along one day—and neither should you.'

Jane sniffed and blew her nose. 'But that's what I keep thinking. I was really sure about Stuart!'

Martha grimaced. She'd privately thought Stuart was painfully pompous and overbearing and that Jane was much better off without him, but all she said gently was, 'Chin up, love. You *will* make some man a wonderful wife one day.'

Which set Jane into a fresh paroxysm of tears for several minutes and it was awfully hard to resist when she got over it bravely but said, 'Tell me more about this man you can't forget, Martha.'

Martha winced inwardly but her voice was quite normal, even casual as she said, 'He was from the UK and out here on promotional tour. His family has produced a very famous liqueur—in France as a matter of fact—for centuries.'

'So was he one of those frightfully upper-crust Englishmen? Or a French Don Juan?'

Martha laughed. 'As a matter of fact he was a Scot, although you wouldn't have known it from his accent. And he wasn't frightfully posh, although...' she paused '...well, you could tell straight away he *was* very upper crust but not because he talked loudly or sounded as if he had a plum in his mouth.'

'I know what you mean,' Jane agreed knowledgeably. 'It's more of an aura, isn't it?'

'Exactly.' Martha glanced at her wryly.

'So what did he look like? Was he wildly handsome? Was he Gallic? I presume if they've been making this stuff in France for centuries there has to be some French connection. Was he dark and dangerous or red-headed and given to wearing kilts?'

Martha laughed. 'No. And yes, there is a lot of French blood in the family apparently but he wasn't dark and dangerous to look at——' She stopped a bit abruptly.

'Well, then—fair but still dangerous?' Jane ventured.

'Not fair either,' Martha said slowly. 'Light brown hair, grey-green eyes, big and tall, thirty-two then——' Again she stopped.

'And devastatingly handsome.' Jane grimaced.

'No. It's hard to pin-point it with some men, isn't it?' Martha mused. 'Some of them seem to have it all without being devastatingly or pin-up handsome. It's something to do with their eyes, I think, and their hands and what they say and how they say it. It's to do with being grown-up and relaxed, yet in command when they need to be— all those things. But he was quite capable of being damning and dangerous.' Yet his body was beautiful, she thought with an odd little wrench of her heart. Strong and fit, wide shoulders...

'So, arrogant but nice in between times? Good-looking without being embarrassingly so? Wealthy and as-sured—definitely dangerous for a nineteen-year-old girl almost straight from the bush,' Jane said softly with such a look of heartfelt concern in her eyes that Martha moved uncomfortably. 'How far did it go and how did it start?' Jane added.

Martha thought ruefully, I'm not going to get away without spilling most of the beans to Jane, having come this far...

'How did it start?' she said slowly—and it was suddenly like being transported back in time...

She could remember exactly how she'd felt the day it had started. How disenchanted with life, how bitter she'd felt about the way fate had provided a crippling drought that had seen her parents have to walk away from their sheep property with nothing. Had seen *her* suddenly transplanted to city life with no qualifications and being reduced to waitressing on a contract basis, at a plush Sydney hotel on that occasion, to promote a famous French liqueur—dressed up, as she thought of it, like a tart. She could feel, almost as if she were wearing it again, the discomfort of a too short skirt, the black and gold sash with the company name on it, the pinch of her obligatory stiletto-heeled shoes as well as her disapproval of black, fish-net stockings.

She could feel again the way men had devoured her with their eyes and how one short, balding man with a paunch had got bolder and touched her intimately. It was almost as if she had once more in her fingers the long-stemmed rose she'd plucked from a vase and had presented to this man, with what she'd hoped was a seductive wiggle, at the same time as she'd raised her foot with every intention of driving her stiletto heel into his shoe and thereby pulverising some of his toes.

She remembered so clearly the tall man who had materialised at her side before she could do it, and taken her arm and marched her out of the room...

'Look here——' She wrenched her arm free.

'No, *you* look here,' he said coolly and cuttingly. 'Who ever gave you the impression that this job provided the opportunity to importune and proposition the guests misled you entirely.'

'I...' Martha closed her mouth and stared up into a pair of grey-green eyes beneath medium-brown hair and was conscious of a good physique beneath a beautifully tailored suit. She was also aware that the man was extremely well-spoken and English, not Australian, and finally that he was appraising her from head to toe with a sort of casual arrogance that was nevertheless quite damning—and it incensed her. 'Is that so?' she said before she stopped to think, and wiggled again. 'Thought that's why I was all dressed up like a tart—what a waste! Still and all——' she realised she'd made her accent deliberately ocker '—I did get your attention. Are you the big boss?'

Those grey-green eyes hardened although he said gently enough, 'May I make a suggestion—why don't you try your services in a brothel?' and walked away.

I don't believe I did that, Martha was still saying to herself several days later, and going hot and cold with the embarrassment of it all; but there was worse to come. A week to the day later she was doing the same kind of job, serving champagne and canapés at an art show this time, in an even more revealing outfit if anything, when who should she encounter but the same man.

What she hadn't bargained for, however, was that the shock of laying eyes on him again would be rather like an electric shock. And making the discovery of how his hands, his clever eyes, his tall, easy carriage and air of assurance—that could so easily turn to such civilised yet doubly damning contempt—how all of those things had been just under the surface of her mind. How, although she hated him, there was something about him that was tormentingly attractive...

What broke the spell was the way he'd taken a glass of champagne, looked her over meditatively and in a way that had made her horribly conscious of her tight skirt and low-cut top, before he'd said only audibly to her, 'Once a tart always a tart, I guess,' and turned away.

Oh, no, you don't! was Martha's first coherent thought, and she deliberately twisted her heel, cannoned into him and, as he turned back, staggered and spilt six full glasses of champagne over him.

'Dearie me—I'm so sorry,' she said with utterly false contrition. 'How could I be so clumsy? Here, let me clean you up!' And she started to dab at him with the napkin she had over one arm.

But he took her wrist and restored her hand to her, murmuring, 'Thank you but I'd rather you didn't—it's a bit public here for the kind of message you're trying to get across, and anyway, perhaps we ought to have dinner first?'

'Dinner?' Martha stared at him. 'First?'

'Before we go to bed,' he said patiently. 'It might just give us the opportunity to exchange names—first,' he added with a grave, totally mocking little smile.

'I...' Martha tossed her head, and her mother or father might have recognised the glint in her blue eyes. 'OK, I'll get my coat!'

'Don't you think you should finish up here before we——?'

'No way! After last week and now this I'm bound to get the sack,' she said prosaically. 'Not that I mind,' she hastened to assure him, and smiled dazzlingly up at him. 'I've got the feeling I'm on to bigger and brighter things. Let's go, mister!'

They went, Martha collecting the sack at the same time as she collected her coat, but she was too angry to care.

They went to a small Italian restaurant that was not, as she'd expected, cheap and nasty, but chic and tasteful. She hid her surprise and made a big thing of discarding her coat and smoothing the low-cut neck of her dress, refreshing her lipstick and combing her hair—things she would normally never have dreamt of doing at a dinner-table.

'What *is* your name, then?' she said brightly when she'd arranged herself to her satisfaction, and was confident that a number of other diners were looking at her with either amused curiosity or raised eyebrows.

'Simon,' he said.

'Pleased to meet you, Simon. I'm Martha.' She stood up and extended her hand. 'You know, I'm not too sure if you're a hotel executive or—well, whatever the hell you are is fine with me.' And she sat down, having shaken his hand vigorously and made her comments audible to all.

'You should be on the stage, Martha,' he replied with a considering look that took in the golden glints in her long fair hair, her deep blue eyes, the curves of her figure—a purely male summing up of a member of the opposite sex that was at the same time quite relaxed.

'Believe me, Simon——' she sat forward with her elbows propped on the table, her cleavage more exposed than it had ever been in her life, and that tell-tale little glint in her eyes again '—I'm sure I *could* be. It's only a matter of being noticed. But you haven't told me what you are.'

He said nothing for a long moment and she just knew he was laughing at her, which incensed her all the more. So that when he did start to tell her she oohed and aahed, appeared suitably impressed, even quite dazzled. And she kept up a flow of bubbling, suggestive chatter throughout the meal until her teeth started to feel on edge.

Then the bill came and he said, 'Well, Martha, would you like another cup of coffee or should we go somewhere more private?'

Whereupon she gazed at him narrowly, laughed harshly and said in a way that she hoped was both world-weary and incredibly common, 'Oh, no, you don't, mister. It takes a bit more than some pasta to get me to bed!' And she stood up and folded herself into her coat with a flourish.

He made no move to rise; he appeared to be amused if anything and he said only, 'How old are you, Martha?'

'Nineteen—what's that got to do with it?'

'Nothing, necessarily,' he drawled. 'Goodnight, then.'

She glared at him and swung out of the restaurant.

Two days later she opened the door of the dingy bed-sitter she rented to find him on the doorstep. And she didn't have to simulate surprise and annoyance; she was in fact quite stunned, then furious, because two days had been ample time to discover how ashamed she felt of herself. Conversely, she was prepared to admit it to no one, least of all Simon Macquarie.

'What are you doing here?' she said rudely. 'And how did you find me?'

His lips twisted. 'It was quite simple. Don't tell me it didn't occur to you, Martha, that all I had to do was make enquiries from the catering company that used to employ you?'

That did it. 'Hey!' She rearranged her features into a cheeky smile. 'You are a bright boy, Simon! Not that I really doubted it. It's just that you've caught me with my hair down.' She had in fact just washed her hair. 'But never mind—come in. And you can tell me,' she added, with a wink, 'what you've thought up now to get me to sleep with you.'

He took his time answering. He looked around the depressing room and then looked her over thoroughly. She was wearing faded jeans and an unexceptional white cotton top and had a towel slung round her neck with which she'd been drying her hair. And at last he said, with a faint quizzical smile touching his lips, 'Before we go into that, can I buy you lunch? I know, I know,' he said wryly, coming to stand right in front her, 'that the price of a meal is not going to do it—I think I might have learnt that lesson.'

'Then what?' she said before she could stop herself.

'You might have to tell me that, Martha. In the meantime, it's a nice day, there are some nice beaches on Sydney Harbour—why don't you bring a swimming costume? We could have a dip before lunch.'

He drove her to Watson's Bay and they did just that—had a swim before a fine seafood lunch at Doyles. And Martha worked conscientiously on her tart act, setting her teeth on edge again but aware that this man aroused two things in her—a troublesome attraction and a deep sense of hostility. But he didn't attempt to touch her and he delivered her home without making any arrangements to see her again.

Suits me, she thought, and for the next few days applied herself diligently to getting another job. The trouble was, she couldn't get Simon Macquarie out of her mind. She kept thinking of his tall body slicing through the water beside her, thinking of the fact that for an Englishman—well, a Scot in fact, as she now knew—he wasn't all pink and lily-white but lightly tanned, and there was something quite beautiful about the strong, lean lines of him that tended to take her breath away. Thinking how adult he was, how obviously cultured and sophis-

ticated, how it would be a pleasure to drop her act and
just be herself, wondering what he'd make of her true
nineteen-year-old self. But when he reappeared on her
doorstep five days later she was furious with herself because of it.

'Oh, it's you again,' she said flatly. It was a chill
evening, her feet were sore from walking to half a dozen
job interviews, none of which held out much hope, and
what lay ahead was an evening alone, making herself
toasted cheese. 'Come up with anything new but lunch
or dinner?'

'Yes, this,' he said quietly, and took the door-handle
out of her hand, closed it and took her in his arms. 'Let's
see how we enjoy kissing each other, Martha,' he said,
barely audibly and with soul-searing little glints of
amusement in his grey-green eyes.

Shock held her suspended for a long moment. Shock
and the feel of him against her body, the way it made
her heart start to pound suddenly, how she shivered involuntarily at the feel of her breasts against the hard
wall of his chest. Shock as she wondered whether she
was not much better than the role she was trying to play
anyway...

It was this thought that made her toss her head and
say, 'OK—let's see what you can do, mister! But only a
kiss, mind.'

'Whatever you say, Martha,' he murmured. And then,
quite a few minutes later, 'How did I do?'

She had to swallow as she stared up into his eyes,
swallow and desperately try to compose herself. Because
what she'd been determined should be a light-hearted,
shallow, give-nothing-away experience had been anything but. Instead, the feel of his fingers on the skin of
her throat and the curve of her cheek before his mouth
met hers had produced a kind of rapture she'd not before

experienced. And the feel of his arms around her had evoked a consciousness of her body that had been quite stunning. And the way she'd melted against him as he'd kissed her had been anything but shallow and light-hearted...

'You did OK,' she said with an effort. 'But hey, I learnt a long time ago not to get too carried away doing this. Could you let me go? My feet are killing me and I'm as hungry as a hound!'

What she saw in his eyes, though, startled her because it appeared to her to be sheer, wicked enjoyment. And he said gravely, 'Of course. I too learnt long ago not to get carried away doing this. Can I say just one thing before I do?'

Martha opened her mouth, closed it then said, 'Fire away, mister, but I haven't got all night.'

He lifted a wry eyebrow. 'My apologies. I was merely going to say that you're... beautiful.'

'Thanks, mate!' But she tore herself away from him before she added, 'You're not so bad yourself. Mind you, I generally go in for Latin types—don't know why; there must be something about dark hair and eyes that turns me on. Care for some toasted cheese? It's about all I've got.'

'No, thank you, Martha. I have a dinner appointment shortly, but perhaps I can help out in the matter of toasted cheese.' And he pulled a fifty-dollar note from his pocket and before she was aware of his intentions opened a gap between the buttons of her cardigan and tucked it into her bra. 'For services rendered,' he said gently, and left.

Martha took a deep, furious breath, plucked the note out and tore it up.

*   *   *

'I don't know why you keep popping up like this,' she said coolly, the next time he called, a Saturday lunchtime.

'Is that your way of saying, Make me an offer I can't refuse or go away?' he queried with a dry little smile.

'Probably. Fifty bucks doesn't go far,' she retorted, and stuck her hands on her hips. 'So what's it to be today?'

He studied her rather pretty floral skirt, thin white jumper and the simple knot she'd tied her hair back in. 'We could go to the races.'

Despite herself a spark of interest lit her eyes, something he obviously noted because he said, 'Do you like the horses?'

'They're OK,' she conceded. 'But I'm not dressed to kill.'

'As a matter of fact I prefer you when you're not,' he said wryly.

'You've never seen me dressed up.'

'Well, no, but I've seen you dressed down, which was what I thought you might have meant—my apologies.'

Martha cast him an angry look beneath her lashes, and went out of her way for the entire afternoon to be as common as she possibly could. But, far from being perturbed, he took her to dinner and took her home without attempting to lay a finger on her.

Which provoked her, although she could have killed herself, into saying, with her hand on the car door-handle, 'I see you're not flashing any fifty-dollar notes around tonight, mister.'

'Would you like me to?'

'Suit yourself.' She shrugged. ''Night, then!' And she slipped out of the car. He made no attempt to stop her.

But over the next few weeks it wasn't always like that. In fact, over the next few weeks she reminded herself of a cat on hot bricks. She would wonder if she'd ever see him again and tell herself she didn't care, but knew she did. She hated the way he could, simply by arriving on her doorstep, make her heart start to pound like a drum and all her nerves quiver. But if he left her without touching her she felt incredibly bereft, even while, when he did kiss her, she tried to go out of her way to let him know she didn't give a damn. Which only amuses him, she reflected once, and had to amend that, Well, not always. Sometimes he gives me back more than I bargained for; sometimes he can be much cleverer and more cutting in what he says, as if there's a darker side to him than he normally displays.

So this is really crazy, she told herself angrily. It's as if I don't know myself any more. Why am I continuing this farce? Because he *believes* it, an inner voice answered, and you can't forgive him for that. And that's even crazier, she thought miserably. But that very evening when he turned up out of the blue and she resolved to have done with Simon Macquarie he all but routed her completely.

'It's a beautiful night. Would you like to drive to South Head? We could watch the moon over the sea.'

'No,' Martha said ungraciously. 'Look here, mister, don't think you can turn up whenever it suits you and expect me to be all sweetness and light and availability.' She had, in fact, just got home herself from the job she'd at last got—curiously with an opposition catering company and doing exactly what she'd been doing when they'd met. Although this time she wore a conservative black dress and a frilly voile apron.

'I see,' he drawled, leaning his broad shoulders against the wall and watching her lazily as she pulled the apron off and threw it over a chair. 'Has one of your Latin lovers claimed you for the night? You know, Martha, there's not a great deal of evidence of men splurging on you.'

'There will be,' she said flatly. 'I just haven't yet met the type who can afford to splurge. Barring you, of course. I don't know why, but I've got the feeling you're something of a miser, Mr Simon Macquarie. Either that or the world's not drinking much cognac these days.' She grimaced. 'And don't,' she said curiously tautly as he moved his shoulders, 'give me that old spiel about concentrating on my beautiful soul.'

'No,' he murmured. 'I won't. To be honest, I'm not sure what kind of a soul you have, Martha, but you do have an exquisite body: skin like smooth satin, lovely bone-structure, beautiful eyes . . . Have you ever been in love?'

'You're joking,' she said scornfully.

'So you don't believe in it?'

'Right at this moment, no.' She turned away with a toss of her hair. 'But don't let that keep you awake at nights!'

'Martha.'

She stiffened as he spoke from right behind her, and said, 'Why don't you just go away?'

'I will, when I've done this—no, don't fight me. We both know now that you quite like it despite the lack of a commercial, paying aspect to it that's obviously dear to your heart.'

She turned and said fiercely, 'You're so clever, aren't you?'

'Not always, no, otherwise I wouldn't be here doing this,' he drawled. 'But since I am . . .'

What prompted her to kiss him back with sudden tense, angry fervour was not entirely a mystery to her. What it led to was . . .

They'd turned no lights on but the moon he'd spoken of was enough to illuminate the old settee they sat on, the curve of her breasts where her button-through dress lay open and had slipped off her shoulders, her front-opening bra laid aside, her head on his shoulder.

Nor did it hide how she trembled as he drew his fingers down her skin and touched her nipples in turn, and how she mutely, at last, raised her mouth for his kiss in a gesture that told its own tale.

But although he did kiss her it was brief and strangely gentle, and then he moved her away and closed the edges of her dress for her, before standing up.

'You don't want to go any further?' she said in a strained, husky voice that wasn't much like her tart voice.

'Yes, I do.'

'Then...?'

'I think we should resist it, Martha,' he said abruptly. 'And I probably don't have to tell you why. I don't make a practice of buying love.'

Martha closed her eyes then glanced down and started to do up her bra and her dress. He said nothing but watched her bent head.

'OK,' she said at last, and stood up herself.

'Just...OK?' he queried drily.

'What do you want me to say?' Some of the colour that had drained from her cheeks was coming back—too much of it, she thought shakily but made an incredible effort. 'Cheers, it's been good to know you— that kind of thing? Why not?'

'Martha——'

But she turned on him suddenly like a tigress. 'Go away, mister. I know that you're trying to tell me I'm not good enough for you—well, you don't have to make a picnic of it! Just go away and stay away and see if I care!'

It was at that moment that her downstairs neighbour who lived with his invalid mother and, despite his dark hair and dark eyes, was a very sober, serious-minded twenty-three-year-old dentistry student, knocked on the door to ask for a couple of teabags, only to get the surprise of his life as Martha opened it.

'Vinny, darling, come in,' she said delightedly. 'Simon's just leaving. Couldn't have worked it out better if I'd timed it with an egg-timer, could I?'

So that's that, Martha said to herself several times over the next days. I'll never see him again, for which I should be profoundly grateful.

But she couldn't help but be shocked by the pain this brought to her heart.

In the event, she did see him again. Three days later, just as she was about to leave for work, he came with a bunch of daisies.

'Oh, now look here,' she began, but discovered her heart was beating erratically with, of all things, hope.

'Could you just ask me in, Martha?'

She hesitated, then with an inward tremor thought, Have I got another chance? Could I tell him how this all happened, how it got out of hand?

'Well, I have to go to work in ten minutes but I suppose so.'

'Ten minutes is all it will take.'

'I could make a quick cup of coffee,' she said, trying to keep her voice steady, trying for anything that would give her courage.

'No. No, thank you. These are for you.' He held out the daisies. 'I'm going home this afternoon. I...' he paused '...I felt I should come and say goodbye.'

'Going home—to the UK?' Her voice seemed to her to come from far off. 'How long have you known that?'

He shrugged. 'Weeks. Martha, there are some things——'

But she took the daisies and clenched her fist around the stems. 'Well! You're a fine one, aren't you, mister? In fact I don't think you're any better than the dirty old men who pinch me on the bottom.'

'That's something I haven't done, you must admit, Martha,' he objected wryly.

'No, you've gone a lot further, *you* must admit, Simon,' she parodied angrily, 'and all in the cause of amusing yourself at my expense. If you must know I think you're a right bastard.'

'Oh, come on, Martha,' he said roughly, 'what did you expect—a diamond bracelet? Or were you trying to hang out for a wedding-ring? Trying,' he emphasised, 'not terribly successfully a couple of nights ago.'

The sheer, soul-searing memory of his rejection that night fired her poor abused heart to fury. 'I hate you,' she gasped, and slapped his face with all the force she was capable of. 'What's more, if all you can afford are *daisies*——' she tore some heads off the offending flowers, totally ignoring the fact that she rather liked daisies normally '—I'm much better off without you.'

'I wonder,' he murmured, and wrested the battered bunch from her grasp, pulled her into his arms and started to kiss her brutally.

'Oh...' she whispered when it was over but could say no more and he didn't release her.

He said instead, 'I came here to try to talk some sense into you, Martha. To tell you to stop this dangerous game you're playing with men, but I guess my earlier conviction was correct—once a tart always a tart.' He smiled unpleasantly as she moved convulsively in his arms and added, 'God help any man who *does* fall in love with you, my little Aussie tart; they'll probably regret the day they were born.'

He released her then, picked up the remnants of his flowers, closed her hand round the tattered bunch and left.

'Oh, Martha...'

Martha came back to the present with a bump as she observed the new tears in Jane's eyes. 'Janey,' she said ruefully, 'you wanted to know—now you do. And I was supposed to be cheering you up, not the opposite!'

'But it's so sad,' Jane protested.

'No, it's not, not any more.' Martha jumped up suddenly and strode over to the window. 'I made a fool of myself; I guess we all do that sometimes but I'm much wiser now.'

'And you just can't forget him, can you?' Jane said softly. 'Is that why there's been no one else?'

Martha was silent for a long moment, then she said wearily, 'Jane, wouldn't you hate to think of yourself reduced to that by a man who was no more in love with you than——? I can't even think of a comparison. So yes,' she said shortly, 'there are some things that are hard to forget.'

'But you didn't give him much of a chance to fall in love with you by the sound of it, Martha,' Jane objected.

'I *wanted* him to, though. I can't tell you how much... Oh, what the hell?' She turned back from the window defiantly. 'The thing was, despite all those wild hopes and dreams, do you know why I kept up that appalling act? Because I knew deep down I was so way out of his league that he would never do more than amuse himself with me.'

'But why?' Jane asked intensely. 'You're beautiful, you've got spirit, you're intelligent, you——'

Martha held up a hand. 'All that's——'

'True!' Jane insisted.

'Pretty girls are a dime a dozen,' Martha said scornfully. 'If I fell by the wayside no one would even notice. The thing is, in those days I was raw,' she said baldly. 'Oh, I don't mean I was uncultured or uneducated but I was certainly unsophisticated,' she added impatiently. 'I had lived all my life on a farm not quite beyond the black stump but not far from it and I only knew about sheep and horses and motorbikes—don't you see?'

'Yes, I do,' Jane replied. 'Not that I agree with raw, except perhaps in your heart.' She stopped and waited.

Martha paced around a bit then tossed her long fair hair back with something like a shiver.

'Displaced, dispossessed, dumped in a big city with no qualifications—of course you were raw,' Jane said quietly. 'With pain and anger, with a huge chip on your shoulder against life and all those who lived it with wealth and ease and assurance—and hungry for love. You were also nineteen,' she added prosaically as Martha cast her a look that told her clearly she was verging on the dramatic, then grinned. 'Don't forget your hormones, ducky. Every magazine you ever read tells you they can make a girl's life hell!'

Martha stared down at her, then her beautiful mouth curved into a reluctant smile and she plonked down on the other end of the settee. 'Promise me something— don't let's lose touch—— Oh, no,' she said helplessly as more tears fell but Jane started to laugh through them and protest that this was the final shower...

It was an eight-hour flight to Singapore, then nearly twelve to London, which gave Martha a lot of time to think, and she sighed several times and wished rather devoutly that she hadn't unburdened herself so to Jane because it had brought it all back and made her wonder how long it would take to forget Simon Macquarie.

I suppose I should take my own words of wisdom to heart, she thought with irony once, and remind myself that if it hadn't been for him I mightn't be where I am today. She laid her head back in the dim cabin as the 747 flew through the night and most people slept around her, and acknowledged that as a direct result of that stormy encounter she'd made a pledge to herself that one day she would be the kind of girl a man like Simon Macquarie could fall in love with. Assured, sophisticated, worldly and certainly not a hot-tempered, rash spitfire who had to wear abbreviated clothes to make a living.

Yet it had been clothes that had got her started towards her goals. Not that she'd even considered modelling clothes as her chosen career; it had chosen her one day out of the blue when at yet another wearying cocktail party a young man with a ponytail and two cameras slung round his neck had touched her on the shoulder and told her in broken English that he could make her into the next Elle MacPherson.

He hadn't, of course. But she'd slowly worked her way into both photographic and catwalk modelling with André Yacob's help, not only photographically but because he'd been able to impart to her some of his almost uncanny love and understanding of fabrics and clothes— and in the process enhanced both their financial positions quite considerably. Which had given her the leeway to go about sophisticating herself, as she thought of it, and to help her parents after the awful tragedy of losing their farm, until they both died within months of each other. That was when she'd decided to fulfil her long-held dream of travelling abroad, and although André had nearly burst into tears and had begged her to stay he'd finally succumbed to her determination and come good in a surprising way. Since she'd had a pair of English-born grandparents and was able to get a work permit, he'd said she might as well keep her hand in at the same time and had written to a friend of his mother's in London—a dress designer, Madame Minter—introducing Martha. Consequently, Martha had an appointment to see Madame Minter the day after she arrived. Although not well-known in Australia, Martha had heard the name and heard it spoken with some reverence.

But if it comes to nothing I'll just start my holiday, Martha thought for the umpteenth time somewhere over India; now why don't you go to sleep?

But even when she did fall asleep she dreamt about Simon Macquarie watching her with that dispassionate, lazy amusement he was so good at, or occasionally with something darker in his eyes and mood that she detected but couldn't understand—as she systematically pulled up beds and beds of daisies . . .

'Well?'

'Dear, oh, *dear*!'

Martha took a deep breath in the rather barn-like studio above an exclusive Chelsea shopfront that featured only one exquisite black silk dress in the window behind the gold scroll on the glass that said simply 'Yvette Minter', and thought, This is all I need! Because, on top of jet-lag, her luggage had been lost, she'd had to cope with her first dizzying experience of London, buy herself some clothes and now, only twenty-four hours after landing, was confronted with this angular, autocratic French woman who'd looked her up and down and, in only slightly less fractured English than André's, commanded her to strut her stuff in a strapless gold evening gown with a huge, billowing, unmanageable skirt. And now she was shaking her head sorrowfully.

Martha's chin came up. 'Look, I know I might not be looking my best, Madame Minter, but I can't be *that* bad,' she said drily.

Madame Minter pulled a scrap of lace from her pocket and applied it to her eyes, still shaking her head sorrowfully.

'OK!' Martha tossed her head. 'Say no more, love!' And she reached behind her to unhook the dress.

'Stop, you foolish child,' Madame Minter commanded, and put the hanky away. 'I only express thees emotion because I wonder where you 'ave been all my life—ah, the 'auteur, the wonderful disdain. I 'ave not seen the like of it for years!'

Martha's mouth fell open.

Madame Minter continued, though, 'And just a leetle touch of vulnerability now and then! Plus the athleticism, the legs, the river of gold 'air, the eyes like deep pansies, the delicate bone-structure so sometimes you will look like a great lady, sometimes like a tomboy. Ah, when I 'ave finished weeth you, Miss Martha, London will never know what 'as heet eet. And we'll sell an awful lot of my clothes, you and I,' she added in brisk, perfectly unaccented English.

'I...I'm...'

Yvette Minter smiled. 'I cultivate my French accent for clients, you know. And sometimes under strong emotion it cultivates me. But tell me, why has André been keeping you to himself all this time?'

'I... Do you mind if I sit down?' Martha said. 'When I've taken the dress off, of course. One thing: I refuse to pout, I always have, but it upsets some photographers.'

'Who's asking you to pout? I loathe pouting women myself!'

Which was how, later, she came to be sitting in a cramped office wearing a silk kimono, drinking strong coffee and listening dazedly to Madame Minter.

'You will be my in-house model,' she was saying. 'I sacked the last one, silly cow. I mean to say——' as Martha blinked '—she actually began to remind me of a stately bovine. She had these large unblinking eyes and she never moved with any...flair. Naturally, when I show my collection,' she went on without pause 'I employ other models, but you will be assured of a place. I have a showing coming up in about a month—dear, oh, dear!'

Martha frowned. 'What?'

'I could have designed it all around you. Never to mind, the next one——'

'Madame, this is all very flattering but——'

'You wish to discuss terms and so on?' Madame eyed her shrewdly. 'What kind of a contract I intend to put you under? One year minimum,' she said succinctly.

Martha blinked. 'Well, I'm not sure,' she said slowly. 'This is supposed to be a holiday, really, and I want to travel——'

'Travel! You will! I take showings abroad. I also intend to make you famous—what's one year when you're——' Madame gestured in a very French way '—twenty-two? My dear Miss Martha, when you're thirty and starting to get leetle lines and your 'air don't 'ave quite same bounce and gravity starts to attract the bust—that's the time to travel!'

Martha had to laugh.

'And this is quite an organisation I've built up,' Madame added proudly. 'You theenk this is some teen-pot outfit?' Her black eyes flashed and her accent came back.

'No, no,' Martha said hastily.

'Thees is good,' Madame said proudly, and switched accents adroitly once more. 'I'm just about to bring out an exclusive off-the-rack range which will be seen in all the best fashion magazines. Seen,' she said dramatically, 'with you inside them. But only if you put yourself in my hands, Martha Winters,' she added sternly. 'You think I'm flattering you? I'm only flattering the raw material.' Martha flinched but Madame flowed on unaware. 'Certainly some fine raw material but still a very great lot to learn. You have somewhere to live? No? You will come and live with me——'

'No, Madame, thank you very much but I must insist that I find my own place.'

Deep pansy blue eyes stared resolutely into snapping black ones and for a moment Martha expected a Gallic explosion but Yvette Minter laughed suddenly. 'I like it, I like it, but you see, you silly girl, I have a perfectly private little basement flat under my house that I will rent out to you for a perfectly normal amount, where you will be able to take your boyfriends without me even seeing them. Mind you, while a certain amount of sex is marvellous for the looks, men do complicate one's life, much as I love 'em.' And an oddly penetrating black glance now came Martha's way.

'Point taken,' she said calmly.

Whereupon Madame raised her eyebrows. 'What does that mean? Don't you like men?'

'It means I'm not looking for any complications at the moment,' Martha said.

'Ah. Hmm. I see. Yes, indeed. So.'

It was Martha's turn to raise an eyebrow.

'I see only that some man 'as 'urt you,' Madame explained, causing a faint tinge of pink to rise to Martha's cheek and causing her to curse herself silently. 'But never to mind,' Madame continued, 'it is you who will be going round breaking hearts soon. In the meantime, are you on, Martha Winters?'

'I...oh, well, they say faint heart never won anything. Yes, I'm on,' Martha heard herself say.

Two weeks later she still felt like pinching herself.

Her basement flat below Madame's elegant Chelsea terrace house, with its window-boxes and tubs of pansies, black enamelled front door with a polished brass knocker facing a quiet leafy garden in the centre of the square, was small but comfortable. And although at first she'd felt a bit like a rabbit living below street level, she'd soon adapted. Who would not, she thought sometimes, to vibrant, stylish, historic Chelsea? And she was gradually finding her way around the King's Road and Fulham Road, Sloane Square, Cheyne Walk and the river.

She'd been to the Natural History Museum, the Albert Hall, Harrods, seen the Grinling Gibbons carvings in the chapel of the Royal Hospital, guided by a delightful ninety-year-old, scarlet-coated Chelsea pensioner, and, rain or shine, she walked up to Hyde Park or Kensington Gardens every morning. For there hadn't been much rain—everyone agreed it was a marvellous spring so far. Of course, she realised there was a whole lot more of London to see, but the truth of the matter was that Yvette Minter might make amazing gestures but she was also something of a slave-driver—Martha had never worked so hard in her life. But she found herself enjoying it, even if she changed clothes fifty times a day or was cajoled, coaxed and screamed at by temperamental photographers, by everyone at Minter's, in fact, all unable to avoid being affected by Madame's histrionics at the forthcoming début of her off-the-rack range.

Then one afternoon, about two weeks after her arrival, Martha donned a blue fitted waistcoat that left her shoulders and arms bare and matched her eyes, a coffee-cream straight silk skirt that fell to just above her ankles and had a slit up the front to above her knees, gold suede shoes, clustered pearl earrings and a chunky gold and pearl bracelet, swept a brush through her hair, which she was leaving long and loose, and walked through to the elegant room where Madame's *haute couture* clothes were shown to clients.

There was no one there apart from Madame herself, who proceeded to walk around Martha, dressed in her inevitable black, but this time definitely a cocktail dress, with her mouth pursed. 'Yes,' she said finally, 'we did right with the 'air; those subtle lighter streaks are very good and a little shorter and all one length so you can toss it around and it settles just a little wild as if some man has been running his 'ands through it but still looking *très bon*—it's very good. And the 'ips under the silk—quite delectable!'

Martha said, 'Thanks,' casually but eyed her warily for she'd learnt that it wasn't only when Madame was with clients or in the grip of emotion that her French accent surfaced; it was also when she was being devious, and she was capable of being extremely devious at times. 'So?' She looked rather pointedly at the empty gilt chairs.

Madame put her hands on her own hips. 'So?' she repeated arrogantly. 'I'm having a little cocktail party at home this evening, just friends, and you are coming, Miss Martha, that's what!'

Martha sighed. 'Madame—look, you've been wonderful about renting me out your basement; you haven't bothered me in the slightest and I hope I haven't bothered you at all—but I think we should keep it that way.'

A flood of genuine French greeted these words which Martha endured stoically, enraging Madame even more until she burst into English, saying finally, 'It's business, you stubborn, ungrateful child!'

'I thought you said it was friends.'

'Friends, yes, but friends who will talk about you—don't you understand anything? Is Australia such a hick place they don't even——?'

'Now look here...' Martha broke in.

'No, *you* look here; it's part of my campaign to make you famous and what do you do? Throw eet een my face!'

Martha grimaced. 'It so happens I hate cocktail parties.'

'This one you won't. That I guarantee. I have never given a party in my life that anyone has hated! Martha Winters—please,' Madame said, changing tack so suddenly that Martha blinked. 'I would like you to come with the very best intentions in my 'eart. I would like everyone to see this fabulous girl who is so soon going to become a sophisticated, wonderful woman——'

'Stop. I'll come,' Martha said, laughing at the same time, as she shook her head a little dazedly.

'So you jolly well ought to,' Madame said severely. 'This place Australia—are they all like you over there, so wary, so stony-hearted, so——?'

'Madame, I said I'd come!'

It was Martha's first glimpse of the first-floor reception-room of Madame's house, and she couldn't fail to be impressed by the looped, draped, tasselled yellow velvet curtains about the tall windows that overlooked the square; by the palest *eau-de-Nil* wall-to-wall carpet that was dotted with exquisite Chinese and Persian rugs; the beautiful, spindly, inlaid pieces of furniture; the flowers and lamps; the vivid pink silk-covered chairs.

But of course it was still an ordeal—to be introduced and overlooked by an ever-growing number of people, to try to make conversation with complete strangers without sounding gauche and, particularly, colonial. I really should have got over these kind of nerves, she told herself once, sipping a very dry sherry. How many times have I paraded before hundreds of strangers? But that's different; I can detach myself then—not something I can do now at the same time as I'm hearing my accent stand out so obviously—not that I care what they think about my accent, so why do I feel like this? Martha asked herself impatiently. Perhaps, she went on to think with a slight shrug, looking round the room suddenly, I can concentrate on the possibility that one day I could own a room like this...

'Miss Martha?'

Martha turned as Madame's voice penetrated her reflections.

'I 'ave a very special guest to introduce you to—my nephew. Simon, this is my new protégé, Martha Winters—is she not stunning?'

Martha froze, her lips parting and her eyes widening as she looked up at the tall man beside Madame who was wearing a beautifully tailored grey suit that sat superbly across his broad shoulders. She took in his quiet air of assurance and authority, his brown hair, his long-fingered hands which had once made her shiver with delight to think of them upon her body—and looked at last into Simon Macquarie's grey-green eyes.

CHAPTER TWO

'WELL, well,' he drawled in that quizzical, amused voice that haunted her dreams, 'we meet again. I wonder if that's pure fate or—something else?'

Two things happened at the same time: Madame burst forth into surprised French and Martha tossed her head and clenched her sherry glass so that her knuckles showed white. Which caused Simon Macquarie to narrow his eyes and cut across Madame's outpourings as he said drily, 'Now, Martha, we've been through this once before. I was remarkably understanding about the champagne but there is a limit—I would drink that sherry if I were you.'

Martha did just that and the next best thing she could think of. She tossed off the last of her sherry, placed the glass down gently on a table, and stalked out with all of the considerable hauteur, disdain and controlled rage she was capable of—leaving the party to fall into a sudden, electrified silence behind her.

Once in the sanctuary of her basement with the door firmly locked, she tore off her earrings and bracelet and flung them down on the kitchen table. She was just in the process of undoing the buttons of her waistcoat when, to her incredulity, she heard a key in the area door and it swung open into her kitchen-cum-sitting-room to admit Simon.

Buttoning herself up with furious, trembling fingers, but aware that he must have seen at least the flesh-coloured silk and lace of her low-cut French bra, she

33

spat, 'How *dare* you! How did you get a key? This is intolerable!'

'It's Yvette's master key,' he said placidly, laying the offending article on the table next to her earrings and bracelet. 'She—er—agreed with me that there was obviously some unfinished business between us.'

'Oh, no, there's not!' Martha flashed, then took a breath as she tried to think, tried to gather herself into some sort of icy composure. 'At least to my mind,' she said in a suddenly cool, reflective voice, 'there's only this, Simon Macquarie. You posed the theory that I'd somehow tracked you down and ingratiated myself with your aunt in a bid to...' She paused, which was fatal as it turned out.

'To re-establish yourself in my life?' he suggested gently, but with such mockery that she winced. 'It did cross my mind, yes.'

'Then you must be mad!' she accused. 'I had no idea she was your aunt, and believe me, if I had, the last thing I'd be doing is working for her.'

'Well,' he murmured with a faint smile, 'you'll have to forgive me for being a little wary of your motives, Martha. But I must say——' that clever, amused gaze roamed up and down her figure '—I have to give you full marks for ambition, my little Aussie tart. This is a rather astonishing climb up the ladder from serving drinks and propositioning guests. Like to tell me how you achieved it?' And with a wryly raised eyebrow he sat down at her kitchen table and picked up the gold bracelet she'd cast down in such a rage, to run it thoughtfully through his long fingers.

Martha had never actually seen red before but what saved her was the sudden, startlingly clear mental picture of what had happened to her the last time she'd slapped this man's face. So she closed her eyes on the red film, very briefly and discreetly filled her lungs with air as she'd been trained to, then sat down opposite him with a shrug and said, 'How do you think? It's amazing what you can achieve—on your back.'

For a long moment their gazes locked, hers not even defiant, she hoped, yet she was momentarily puzzled by the tinge of scepticism she thought she saw in his; then it was gone and she wondered if she'd imagined it.

But he said abruptly, 'So that part of it *was* always true?' And there was no mistaking the cold disgust in his eyes now.

'Of course. Did you ever doubt it?' Martha asked sweetly, despite the strange mixture of hurt and the feeling that she was tumbling down a mine-shaft—by her own hand but unable to stop herself. 'Perhaps I was a bit...rough in those days. Is that what made you have doubts? Well, I'm much, much more experienced now, Mr Macquarie. Would you like a demonstration?'

He relaxed all of a sudden. 'No, thank you, Miss Winters. I think I could live without it. No,' he mused. 'What activated certain doubts was the sometimes undoubted genuineness of your—rages. But I guess we're all wrong from time to time. Does my aunt know how you operate?' he asked drily.

I've gone too far—I've done it *again*! Martha found herself thinking dully as she coloured a little. Why does this man *do* this to me? Then she stood up abruptly, swung her hair defiantly and said equally drily, 'No. In fact I've turned over a new leaf. Now I've got this far it would be silly to...well, I guess you know what I mean.'

'Acquire a sleazy reputation?' he suggested softly.

'Yes,' she said shortly, but couldn't prevent herself from shooting him one brief, blazing glance.

His lips twisted. 'Well, I hope you succeed. And I hope you don't find it too difficult to live without,' he added, standing up himself.

Martha knew exactly what he meant as his gaze drifted up and down her again as if he could see beneath the blue crêpe and the coffee silk and she was reminded with deadly accuracy how it felt to have his hands on her body, but he didn't leave a thing to chance. He moved towards her and stopped only inches away so that she was assailed by everything about him that she'd always found so tormentingly attractive: his height and the width of his shoulders; the slight tang of a lemony aftershave and the sheer male smell; the hard planes and angles of his fit, lean body that she'd secretly so admired. And she recalled the rapture of being kissed and held by him and how her heart had beaten and her skin shivered of its own accord, how her nerves had leapt...

She swallowed as she tried to gaze up unaffectedly into his eyes and remembered that he'd always been more than a match for her, and not only physically. She remembered, too, how he'd looked into her eyes, often after a passionate embrace, with that assessing, clever amusement lurking in the greeny depths of his and that wry, ironic twist to his lips and just sometimes with a more deadly kind of mockery.

She opened her mouth, desperate for something to say to break the unbearable tension of the moment, but he spoke first. 'Live without sex, I mean,' he murmured, and smiled as she trembled suddenly. 'It should be interesting, Martha, to see how you cope. And I suppose one can't altogether blame you for working your way up the ladder on your back when there are places on your body where your skin is like silk and there are curves and hollows so well arranged and designed, so erotic and sensitive, it's...' he paused '...almost a crime to find that you haven't got the heart and soul to go with them. But——'

'Get out,' she whispered, rigid and white to the lips.

'Just going. Good luck...'

'Look, Madame, I apologise for walking out of your party but if you want to sack me for it that's fine with me.'

Yvette Minter threw up her hands. She was wearing a colourful, stiffened-silk dressing-gown and she'd descended the area steps and knocked Martha up only moments ago. It was the morning after the party, a Sunday morning, and about nine o'clock. 'Why did I *know* you would say something like that to me?' she demanded in clearly aggrieved tones. 'Can you not even offer me a cup of coffee at this horrendous hour of the day?'

Martha shrugged and turned to the stove where a percolator was bubbling gently. 'If you like.' She poured two mugs.

Madame glanced at Martha's bent head during this process but uncharacteristically said nothing for a time as she sat down and arranged the rich folds of her gown around her.

'There.' Martha pushed a mug across the table and after a brief hesitation sat down herself.

'*Merci*.' Madame smiled faintly and pursed her lips.

This caused Martha to wonder what was coming and it was as if Madame guessed her thoughts, because she said lightly, 'I was just thinking—such a difference! Last night you were all fire and elegance; today you are like a teenage girl.'

Martha grimaced down at the floral patterned leggings and voluminous T-shirt she wore. 'So?'

'That's another thing—how many times you say, "So?" to me, like so.'

'Sorry. I guess what I'm trying to say is this. If I've blown my chance, if I've disgraced myself thoroughly and you can't see any hope of retrieving things and making me famous——' there was a tinge of irony in her voice '—you only have to tell me straight.'

'Martha,' Madame reproved, 'why are you so prickly?'

'It's the way I'm made, I guess.' Martha shrugged.

'OK, I believe you, but what makes you think you disgraced yourself last night? All you did was add a bit of spice and mystery to the image. Believe me, to walk out on Simon—even to want to, let alone to do it—is a gesture not many girls make.'

'Then they should,' Martha said before she could stop herself. 'I'm sorry if he's your nephew but he——' She stopped abruptly.

'Go on,' Madame said, her black eyes fairly snapping with curiosity.

Martha bit her lip and thought, Shades of Jane...'No—uh—well, the least said, the soonest mended, I'm sure. Unless *he*...' She stopped and looked directly at the other woman.

'He has said nothing. *Nothing*,' Madame emphasised. 'Well, beyond that he met you three years ago in Australia. He has left me totally in the dark in other words—which is extremely frustrating for a woman like me,' she added with complete honesty. 'Mind you, it's not hard to guess that you two—er—had something going; the air nearly sizzled around you. What a shot in the eye for Sondra Grant.' She sighed with obvious pleasure.

'Who's she?'

Madame opened her eyes very wide. 'His fiancée— well, his unofficial fiancée—you didn't know?'

'I don't know anything about him, other than that he can be an absolute——'

'Then I will tell you.' Madame sat forward eagerly, and took not the slightest notice of Martha's protest. 'He is the son of my late 'usband's brother—in reality we bear the same name but I chose to use my maiden name for my business. Now you think it's strange that I should have married a Scot? Not at all; the Macquaries 'ave married French women often; the family is half French anyway because——'

'I know about the liqueur,' Martha said drily. 'That's how we met in Australia—at a cocktail party but serving liqueur instead.'

'Ah!' Madame looked suddenly enlightened then she became serious again. 'But do you know that Simon has literally saved the family company from fading into oblivion and turned it into a highly profitable concern again? Because he is a brilliant businessman—dynamic. Why, without his advice even I wouldn't be where I am today and——'

'Madame——' Martha stood up '—I'm really not interested. I'm sorry——'

'So he was the one?'

'The one what?'

'Who 'urt you, Martha. Look——' Madame became angry at last '—don't take me for a fool, Mees Winters!'

'I'm not!' Martha denied. 'But he is your nephew— Oh, this is impossible,' she whispered suddenly, and was horrified to find she had tears welling. Tears because she could see a new life she'd just begun to believe in shattering before her eyes.

'What's that got to do with it?'

'What's what got to do with it?' Martha asked impatiently, dashing at her eyes with the back of her hand.

'That he's my nephew?' Madame said with more of her old arrogance.

'*Everything*, I should imagine. I hate him, he...despises me, and I couldn't even begin to tell you how much. We could be tripping over each other all the time, but you obviously admire him tremendously and——'

'So you think I automatically take his side, Miss Martha?'

'Yes!'

Madame stood up and arranged her robe regally around her. 'Then you do not even begin to understand me, Martha Winters,' she said chillingly. 'I do not only design exquisite clothes but I am a very fine judge of character as well as human nature. I'm also a Frenchwoman through to my bones and as such I know a lot about men, so I would never dream of saying, This man is my nephew therefore he must be all honour and virtue. No. Instead I say to myself, This is a man, first and foremost, and we all know what bastards men can be sometimes—this is what I say!'

Martha stared at her then sat down abruptly, dropped her face into her hands and started to laugh a little wildly. 'But you hardly know me from a bar of soap!'

'True,' Madame conceded. 'But I like you. So, hate Simon if you wish to. It will not affect me. But it also might not deceive me entirely.'

Martha looked up. 'What do you mean?'

'*Chérie*,' Madame said kindly, 'you do not deceive me for one *moment*. However, before you get your 'ackles all in a knot again, I will say not one word more!' And for once in her life she didn't.

Neither did Martha. For the simple reason that she rather felt as if she'd had all the stuffing knocked out of her.

But she was back at work the next morning and Madame's avowed liking for her didn't prevent Madame

from putting her through a gruelling day, or from telling
her she looked like a sack of potatoes in a certain outfit.

It was almost a fortnight before she saw Simon
Macquarie again, then she saw him twice in two days.

The first time was at a pub in Fulham Road. It was
a hot, dry Friday with an uncharacteristically merciless
sun beaming out of an English sky. It had been a torrid
week work-wise as well and she was only too happy to
escape the salon during her lunch-hour and the depths
of the pub had looked cool and inviting so she'd ordered
a Caesar salad and a glass of iced tea. It had taken a
few minutes to notice that Simon was among a group
on the other side of the room, mostly men in business
suits and with briefcases but one eye-catching girl with
them, sitting next to him.

Sondra Grant? Martha wondered. Or a business as-
sociate? Because, for all that her bobbed, dark, shining
hair, pale olive skin, slightly exotic bone-structure and
deeply red painted mouth were rather stunning, she wore
a plain black suit and white blouse, a man's watch on
her wrist, and, as Martha's eyes rested on her, delved
into a black leather briefcase and withdrew what looked
like a formal document from it that she handed to Simon.
Then again, Martha mused, watching the way their
shoulders touched as they scanned the document, not
altogether business associates probably...

All of which, to her disgust, had the effect of turning
the salad she'd been enjoying to sawdust. She got up
and left not long afterwards, taking a detour around the
room so she wouldn't come within recognising distance,
hopefully.

It was her Saturday off the next day, still hot and
bright, and after sleeping in for once in her life, then
doing her chores at home, she walked up to South
Kensington where she shopped, browsed for an hour in

a fascinating bookshop, and finally walked home via
Sydney Street and St Luke's Parish Church. What
prompted her to stop as she realised there was about to
be a wedding she never knew. But there were a few other
people standing at the iron railings and it was undoubtedly going to be a posh wedding, judging from the
Rolls and Mercedes coming and going and the morning
suits and fancy hats. So she stayed to watch, telling
herself she had nothing else to do anyway and it was
interesting to see the clothes and try to work which were
designer ones and which were not.

Finally the bride arrived and she turned out to be a
short, plump, pink-cheeked girl in a plain, beautiful silk
dress but a mixture of nerves and stars in her eyes. And
Martha saw her take a deep breath then turn to go into
the dark, cavernous recesses of the church on the arm
of her father with only two little page boys behind her.
But for some reason Martha also found herself unusually touched as she bent down to pick up her shopping
bags. By the blue of the sky and the green of the grass
on the other side of the railings, the beautiful old honey-
coloured stone of the church—and a plain girl taking a
momentous step in her life.

So she got a double shock to find Simon Macquarie
in khaki cotton trousers and a blue open-necked shirt
standing right behind her, even picking up one of her
bags himself—double because she had a lump in her
throat that would be a dead give-away if she opened her
mouth. But perhaps he saw something in her eyes because he raised an eyebrow and said, 'I wouldn't have
taken you for the kind of person that cries at weddings,
Martha.'

She cleared her throat but it was still in a slightly husky
voice that she replied, 'No? Just goes to show, doesn't
it? Perhaps I'm regretting lost opportunities, that kind

of thing. What,' she enquired coolly, having regained complete control of her voice, 'are you doing here?'

'I live around here.'

'I might have known.'

'What's that supposed to mean? By the way, I saw you yesterday, having a single, chaste lunch.'

'Saw me? But I——' Martha closed her mouth quickly.

He smiled slightly. 'Took pains to be invisible? I know. Perhaps I have a certain sensitivity—about you.'

'After three years?' Martha said drily. 'I find that very hard to believe. If you'd mind handing over my meat and groceries, I'll get going.'

'Oh, I'll walk you home,' he said blandly. 'It's a lovely day.' But he made no move. Instead a rather thoughtful greeny grey gaze took in her floral leggings, T-shirt and blue canvas shoes.

'What *now*?' Martha demanded through clenched teeth.

'Two things,' he drawled. 'You look ridiculously young and untouched in that gear but——' he overrode her '—I was just wondering what kind of a scene you were going to make to—dispel the illusion.'

'Well, you're in for a surprise,' Martha said conversationally, having fought a very brief battle with herself and decided she would rather die than afford him the satisfaction of a scene, despite the fact that it might be playing right into his hands. But then he'll be in for a shock there too, she vowed as she continued sweetly, 'Do you know, and I'm surprised——' she started to stroll along, swinging her bags '—really surprised no one's told you this, but men who think they know everything are the most *boring* men on earth.'

He laughed but said only, 'Come and have a drink. We could expand this theory of yours——'

'No!'

'Not even at the Chelsea Farmer's Market just across the road? You'd be quite safe. Did you think I was planning to lure you back to my house? Now I don't think *that* would be safe at all, Martha,' he murmured. 'For either of us.' And with one quizzical look that seared her to the depths of her soul he simply crossed the road with her meat and groceries still in his hand and walked through the entrance to the colourful market.

'Not such a bad idea after all,' he said lightly after she'd eaten a hamburger and was sipping a glass of chilled white wine. 'Mind you, I must admit it's often hard work to get models to eat lettuce leaves, let alone hamburgers, but you didn't finish your lunch yesterday, did you?'

Martha narrowed her eyes against the sun and refused to be provoked. 'Nor had I had lunch today.'

'I know the feeling.' He stretched his long legs out and put his hands behind his head. 'Well?'

'Well? I'm not sure what you're trying to say. That I'll never make the top if I go on eating hamburgers, which was entirely your suggestion by the way, or——'

'No, I was merely pointing out that we can relax in each other's company.'

'So we can,' she murmured. 'Although I'm not sure what the point of it is.'

He grinned. 'Perhaps even old adversaries like us, if you can call it that, can't keep fighting all the time. How's work?'

Just keep cool, Martha warned herself. 'Your aunt is highly temperamental so that I doubt if working for her is ever a peaceful experience, but the new range, the off-the-rack one, is quite stunning. I'm enjoying it despite all the drama,' she confessed.

'I think she's enjoying having you,' he commented. 'She said to me the other day, "Ah, that one, she 'as a mind of 'er own!"'

Martha looked across at him. 'You were discussing me with her?'

'Not at all. Your secrets are quite safe with me.'

'So how did I come up?' Martha enquired drily.

'She was showing me some of the photography for the new range.'

'Is that all she said?' Martha bit her lip.

'Yes. Why?'

'Nothing.' She sat up. 'Thanks for lunch but I'd better get going.'

'Tell me something before you go, Martha. Have you made any friends?'

'No, as you so rightly observed, I'm still managing to stay chaste.' She directed him a blue gaze full of irony.

'So you're going home to wash your hair and spend this lovely Saturday evening watching television?' he said with a mocking little glint in his eye. 'What a waste; but there are not only men friends to be had in this world.'

'I am aware of that,' Martha said, counting to ten beneath her breath as she fished in her purse and started to count out the exact money for her lunch and wine. 'And no, I haven't made any other friends as yet, but it will come, I'm sure. It also seems to me that sworn enemies such as you and I can't help fighting, so I was right, there seems little point in this kind of truce, besides which it's a bit exhausting. But never let it be said I'm *cheap* in the matter of free lunches.' And she pushed the pile of coins in front of him, adding with what she hoped was insouciance and her best Australian accent, 'Good-day, mate.'

But as she went to turn away he caught her wrist, and said, so that only she could hear in the colourful throng enjoying the sun in the open air. 'You won't last, you know, Martha. If I hadn't had my wits about me you'd have gone to bed with me three years ago.'

But Martha stayed to hear no more. With an upward chop of her wrist she broke his grip, gathered her bags and strode away.

'Ah-ha!' Madame said with deep satisfaction a few days later, days during which Martha had reminded herself of an angry tigress lashing her tail, but it hadn't appeared to affect her image.

They were taking a rare coffee break together in Madame's untidy little office and Madame was immersed in a newspaper—she adored the tabloids, magazines and, as well as being a born gossiper at times, read the gossip columns avidly.

'Someone you know?' Martha asked wryly.

'Yes. You. They are starting to sit up and take notice. And, just as I told you, this thing you 'ave with Simon is adding spice and mystery, *chérie*. Did I not think to tell you that the Farmer's Market might not be the best place to cross spears with 'im if you didn't want the whole world to notice?'

'Swords,' Martha said, but a trifle hollowly, and added, 'Oh, hell.'

'So the feud continues,' Madame continued with a quick, gleeful glance at her in-house model. 'But it also says, "Who is this exquisite girl seen, but not for long, with cognac tycoon Simon Macquarie last Saturday in the Chelsea Farmer's Market? We believe Madame Minter may have been keeping her under double wraps..." Ah, but the wraps are coming off!' Madame said.

'I... Hang on, I didn't realise you wanted that kind of publicity.'

'What's wrong with it?' Madame queried innocently.

Martha gritted her teeth. 'OK. What do you mean about the wraps coming off, then?'

'Just that we start to do some socialising: Ascot, Wimbledon, that kind of thing. Now we're not going to have the kind of fight we 'ad over the cocktail party, are we, Martha Winters? After *all* I've done for you?'

Martha opened her mouth but Madame continued forcefully, 'Is it such a lot to ask that you wear *my* clothes where all the rich women and girls will see them and find they crave, to the bottom of their souls, a Yvette Minter outfit? Is it really too much to ask—while at the same time you will be meeting and mixing with the cream of society, all these rich and famous people, people you 'ad no 'ope of meeting at 'ome? Don't even be surprised if you find a rich, 'andsome 'usband with a title, and who would you have to thank? Me!'

Martha put her hands over her ears as much from a surfeit of dropped aitches. 'I don't want a titled husband and I'm sure they wouldn't want me——'

'Of course you do! We all do,' Madame said scathingly. 'Do you know what I was when I met Simon's uncle? A machinist in a garment factory—but look at me now. I have a box at Ascot, my 'ouse, a million-pound business, and you know why? Because I used my 'ead as well as my looks. Besides which,' she said in suddenly gentler tones, 'think what a shot in the eye it would be for Simon, since you hate him so much.'

'I thought I was supposed to be a shot in the eye for his fiancée,' Martha said a little wildly.

Madame opened her hands. 'Whatever.'

'Is she dark and some kind of a professional person?' I don't believe I asked that, Martha thought distraughtly.

But Madame nodded. 'An accountant with the firm that does his auditing. Very forthright and businesslike but quite attractive if you like brainy, bossy women.' She shrugged. 'Once again, Martha Winters, are you on?'

So Martha was seen at the races in a stunning, short-skirted navy blue silk suit that hugged her figure and a big hat that many women simply stopped, stared at and sighed wistfully over. She was seen eating strawberries and cream at Wimbledon in a yellow tube top and a three-quarter-length full skirt the colour of string and another hat, this time straw and decked with flowers that had nearly the same effect, although its effect on Simon Macquarie, who happened to be at Wimbledon that day, was a little different. As they approached one another he stopped and prevented her from sweeping past by simply standing right in her path.

He was dressed casually and the sunlight was turning strands of his thick brown hair to gold and doing the same to the hairs on his arms. He looked relaxed and perfectly at home as he examined her smooth shoulders and the curve of her breasts beneath the strapless yellow top then said gently, 'Why, Martha, you are exhibiting your wares today.'

Martha clenched her teeth because her heart had started to beat erratically just at the sight of his tall figure and she couldn't understand why it should for a man who could be so cruel and wound her so easily with a few mockingly gentle words and a wry little smile. And she turned on her heel after one tense, explosive moment and walked the other way.

She was seen at the theatre, at lunch, at the Trooping of the Colour, on the river in a private launch, at shows and showings, music festivals—and Madame's clippings began to mount up. They generally began with, 'Australian model, Martha Winters, showing off the best of British fashion again,' or words to that effect, but they gradually became more personal: 'Unusually reserved Australian model, Martha Winters, who never bothers to hide her accent when she can be got to talk and refuses to pout, apparently...' et cetera. Or, 'Australian model Martha Winters actually confided that she was more at home on a motorbike—what a metamorphosis!' Of which Madame didn't approve at all as it happened—the bikie image, as she put it.

'I didn't *confide* that as if I was proud of being some sort of bikie!' Martha protested, and added, 'I can't understand why everyone is so interested in every word I utter—or more particularly don't utter for that matter—or why people look at me the way they do.'

'Now, Martha, I know you're not vain—in fact you're refreshingly the other way—but you're not stupid,' Madame said with irony.

'No——' Martha frowned '—but I just sometimes wonder if there's not more to it. I don't know how to explain it but—well, take that article you're reading,' she said, and plucked the offending paper that had started off its article with references to motorbikes out of Yvette's hands. 'I merely happened to mention to a wild-looking young man who rolled up on a Harley Davidson to that overly contrived picnic at Henley you sent me on that I liked his bike. He was the only one I could find to talk to. Everyone else was paired off——' she shrugged '—but this is what they write.' She started to read the rest of the article.

'"Martha Winters, who is so beautiful and doing a great job of promoting Yvette Minter's clothes, is also something of an enigma. She never seems quite at home—is she still longing for the Antipodes? It's certainly surprisingly hard work to get her to relax.

Nor, as is so often the case with these stunning young women, does there seem to be a beau in tow, or three or four. One has heard rumours of Simon Macquarie but they involved him getting his marching orders, apparently—sorry, Simon! In fact, the only man I've seen Matchless Martha talking with any degree of ease to is Ricky Asquith-Font, and it's rumoured they discussed motorbikes, a well-known passion with the heir to the fiefdom of——''

'*What*?' Madame sat bolt upright.

'"Please, Martha,"' Martha read on, '"can't you put us out of our misery? We've all got our tongues hanging out"—that's disgusting,' Martha said, and threw the paper on to the floor. 'If you expect me to—— What's wrong?'

'You didn't tell me it was Ricky Asquith-Font!'

'I didn't know. What's so riveting about it? Haven't you read the article anyway?'

'I hadn't finished it before you tore it out of my hands. Martha, his father is an earl!'

'So what?' Martha said with a shrug. 'He's only a boy. And a bikie at that,' she added with a wryly lifted eyebrow.

'Oh-ho! And you're such an expert? He's twenty-three, one year older than you. Moreover,' Madame persisted with considerable frustration, 'he seems to be the only man in the entirety of this city of London that you get along with!'

'It was never,' Martha said calmly, 'in my contract nor in any way mentioned verbally that I should set this city of London alight with rumours of who I was sleeping with or not. In fact it was you yourself who told me what a complication men can be.'

'I don't expect you to go to bed with all of them but——'

'Thank you,' Martha said politely.

'But not to be interested in any of them! That is . . . I am without words!'

'Well, I'm not,' Martha murmured. 'Perhaps you should recall that you're a designer of exquisite clothes—not a broker of sleeping partners.'

Which, of course, provoked a row of such proportions, with Martha losing her temper for once too, that all of Madame's long-suffering staff were confident enough to predict that Matchless Martha would be getting *her* marching orders, talking of such things . . .

She didn't.

After three days of such arctic treatment that it was hard to believe the sun was shining outside, she took the plunge herself, saying directly to Madame, 'If I offended you, I apologise. But my point remains.'

'Remains! Your point! All I was trying to do was say, Here's a start. One young man you can talk to, one young man who could set the ball rolling—what is so terrible about that? So terrible that you accuse me of *cross commercialism*?' She rolled her Rs mightily.

Martha sighed. 'I thought, after reading that article, that I might not be—well, turning out the way you'd hoped, and that's why you got so angry. That the mystery and fire, all of which is so bound up in selling clothes, had become just a mundane Aussie girl who can be a bit like a block of wood when it comes to men. But you see, I can't change that.' She shrugged and added, 'It's also nobody's business but mine.'

Madame drew a breath through her narrow nostrils and Martha steadied herself for another explosion. But Madame then sat down rather abruptly and said, 'Simon? He is responsible for all *this*? Believe me, I am no broker of sleeping partners but I was so sure that once you got over your nerves you would start to live and laugh and love a little like any normal girl of your age. You are made for love, Martha.'

Martha said nothing.

'Then I'll tell you something else—I am selling more clothes than ever before. Look around you. Go to the factory, look at these orders——' She thumped a pile of papers. 'Are we not snowed under?'

'Then...' Martha stared across at her, momentarily arrested. 'I didn't realise...' she said a bit lamely, and frowned. 'Why did you get so angry?'

'Because I like you although I often ask myself why,' Madame said sardonically.

'Not because I seem to be turning men away rather than the opposite?'

'Turning them away with their tongues hanging out!'

'I hate that——'

'And because you won't take any advice!' Madame said frustratedly. 'How can you not expect me to say 'orrible things when I try to 'elp you build a life like mine for you and you don't—you won't... I don't know!'

'You're not——' Martha stopped.

'Say it!'

'Perhaps not——'

'After a broker of sleeping partners and crass commercialism, what can be worse?' Madame enquired acidly.

'Hankering after a daughter, then?'

Black eyes stared into blue ones then Madame stood up and sighed. 'I couldn't have picked a worse one to vent my latent maternal instincts on, could I? It's true, I do feel the lack of children sometimes, but it is a matter of extreme surprise to me, the way I worry about *you*, Martha Winters,' she added crossly, then grimaced. 'But the thing is you remind me of myself at your age. I was also fiery and I had a chip on my shoulder and was often angry.' She shrugged.

'Well, I think it's just about the nicest thing anyone's said to me,' Martha said gently.

'So, we forgive each other?'

'Until the next time,' Martha said with a wry grin.

'And you will wear this dress to the Fashion Guild summer ball?' Madame swept aside a curtain. 'No one, I repeat no one will mistake you for a block of wood once they've seen you in it,' she said craftily.

Martha examined the dress critically. 'It's beautiful,' she said finally with a tinge of surprise, 'but——'

'Martha!'

'Oh, OK.'

CHAPTER THREE

I MUST have been mad, Martha thought gloomily as she stood delivered, relieved of her wrap and awaiting introduction beside Madame and her escort, a distinguished silver-haired gentleman of whom Madame seemed particularly fond. Indeed, Martha had seen the same gentleman twice, departing the house in a black BMW at a very early hour of the morning. Mad to come without a partner, she decided... mad to come at all!

Then the sonorous accents rolled forth. 'Madame Minter, Sir Oswald Henry, Miss Martha Winters.'

Nor, as she stepped forward with all the outward supple ease and unconcern of a professional model, did the little ripple of admiration that lapped around the room console her much. It's more for the dress than me anyway, she mused. It is, probably, the most exquisite gown I've ever worn. And she caught sight of herself in a long panel of mirrors and sighed inwardly.

It was not, as Madame had taken pains to point out to her, the typical strapless taffeta with a full skirt so beloved of typical débutante types. It was quite the opposite, in fact: a suit, with a short-sleeved, high-necked, intricately beaded and sequinned jacket sewn on to a fluid silk crêpe that moved with every move she made so that the soft jade-green of it all shimmered and flowed in rivers of light. The skirt was the plain jade silk crêpe, quite straight, with only a discreet slit up the back, the shoes covered with matching fabric and with sequinned heels. It was, apart from the fabulous beading and sequins, an almost austere design, yet it highlighted every curve of her body beneath it and fitted so well, sat so lightly, it was like a second skin and gave her the freedom of movement only a marvellously constructed garment could. And it caused every other gown in the room to sink into insignificance.

'Done it again!' Madame whispered gleefully into Martha's ear. 'Your 'air looks good too, up like that. Don't be at all surprised if some man wants to take it down or tear your outfit off. I say this only to warn you because I would not be at all 'appy if someone tore that dress.'

What this actually did was make Martha laugh and therefore relax a bit, so that when someone touched her elbow, and she turned and discovered Ricky Asquith-Font standing there looking somewhat pole-axed, despite his flamboyant dinner-suit and red velvet bow-tie, despite his entirely modish hairstyle of short back and sides and long, straight, flopping forelock which he raked back nervously, she took pity on him and asked him how his Harley Davidson did.

A couple of hours later, Madame whispered into her ear again. 'I told you! Did I not tell you? You *can* enjoy yourself if you just let go a little.'

Martha grimaced but the truth was she was a little flushed; she was never for a moment without a dancing partner and she was enjoying herself. And later she even heard one young man say, 'Have you seen? The ice maiden has come alive! And all at the hands of our beloved Ricky. What's he got that I haven't?'

'If you believe what you read, an affinity with motorbikes—and an earldom round the corner,' his companion said drily.

But Martha only smiled slightly. She was behind them, wending her way back to Ricky's table from a visit to the powder-room, but the smile died as she looked up

into the eyes of a man suddenly blocking her path—
Simon Macquarie.

Neither of them said anything for a moment. Truth
to tell, Martha discovered, she because the sight of him
in a dinner-suit and snowy white shirt almost took her
breath away. Then there was the way he allowed his gaze
to drift over her, taking in the fresh, frosted lips, the
tidied gleaming hair, the way a pulse in a creamy hollow
at the base of her throat just above the jade neckline
started to beat and the way she clenched her hands
involuntarily.

Then, when he spoke, she knew he'd overheard the
conversation she just had, because he said, quite casually, 'He's too young for you, you know, Martha, despite the earldom.'

Her eyes came up, her breath quickened and she tossed
her head. 'And I'm beginning to think you were always
too old for me, Simon. May I get past?'

'Not until we've had a dance,' he murmured. 'I'm
getting a little tired of featuring in the gossip columns
as the guy Martha Winters is always walking out on—
such as now.'

'If you didn't *say* . . . if you didn't always bait me . . .
If I've hurt your pride, I'm glad,' she finished coldly,
at last articulating one coherent thought.

His lips twisted but he merely took her hand. 'OK—
do it again, Martha,' he invited. 'You'll have everybody
absolutely captivated and we'll be splashed over everything readable tomorrow.'

She bit her lip furiously but didn't resist as he led her
on to the floor and took her into his arms. She did say
suddenly, 'All right, two can play this game!' and smiled
past him with every appearance of being entirely at ease
as she added barely audibly, 'You asked for it—let's see
what they make of this!' She started to match her steps

and her body to his, and her highly developed sense of rhythm to the beat of the music—only to find his sense of rhythm was as good as hers, and that they danced together as if they'd been made for each other.

'I'm not sure what you were trying to prove,' he said once as he turned her expertly and drew her back into his arms. 'That I'd fall over my feet?' He smiled quizzically into her eyes before he released her for another spinning turn.

'I thought...I thought you weren't even *here*,' she said disjointedly as her feet flew to the music.

'I came late.'

'With Sondra Grant?' The words were out before she could help herself and she was left to wish she'd bitten her tongue.

He raised an eyebrow. 'No, as a matter of fact. What do you know about Sondra?'

'Nothing. Nor do I want to,' she replied less than truthfully. 'But I couldn't help wondering what she must be making of the gossip columns. I hope you've reassured her.'

'Oh, I don't think she's in any need of reassurance. She was amused if anything. You dance extremely well, Martha,' he said as the music came to a climax and he spun her around and around one last time.

'Thank you,' she panted, coming to rest at last squarely in his arms where he'd fully intended that she should. 'Don't——' she also said, and bit her lip. Let me go, she'd been going to say but only because she was dizzy—as he'd also fully intended perhaps?

'I won't,' he murmured, and waited gravely as her breathing steadied and the room steadied and couples began to leave the floor. Then, with deliberate intent, he lowered his head and kissed her firmly, full on the mouth, as her lips parted and her eyes widened then darkened; but before she could do any more he released her and, with the full force of that darkness she sometimes saw in him, bowed slightly then walked away, taking the handkerchief from his top pocket to remove any traces of her lipstick as he went—leaving her standing virtually alone in the middle of the floor, staring after him, before she coldly, proudly, blindly, but few people realised it, swung round herself, walked back to Ricky's table and sat down only moments before her knees would have buckled.

'This is a little extreme, isn't it?'

Martha's head jerked up from her packing and she stared incredulously at Simon Macquarie standing at her bedroom door. It was the next morning and another Sunday. 'I might have known,' she said furiously. 'Go away!'

'Known that Yvette would call me in?' He leant his broad shoulders negligently against the door-frame. He was wearing his khaki trousers again with a navy blue pullover over a green shirt and he looked big, disturbingly dispassionate and quite capable of—anything, she thought with a little inward shiver. 'She is distraught,' he agreed. 'She says you're planning to go straight back to Australia. She says I've ruined a fabulous career. She says I've ruined you,' he added meditatively.

'Oh, no, you haven't,' Martha denied coldly.

'Then why this agony of remorse or whatever it is?' he queried drily.

'Is that what you think it is?' Martha said through her teeth. 'How wrong can you be?' she marvelled. 'Because I'll tell you what it is. It's pure disgust. With you particularly. But I'm not going to stay here and be written about like a lump of meat.' Her voice choked briefly so she tossed her head and threw some more underclothes into her suitcase.

'Actually,' he drawled, 'I thought you came out rather well this morning. The gist of the gab seemed to be that Simon got his own back at last but they all felt sorry for you. "Did Martha the Magnificent—and she was truly magnificent last night—deserve to be treated like this? What goes on between these two?"' he quoted as he lifted a newspaper from the floor that held a picture of Martha at her most vulnerable moment, looking after him as he left the dance-floor.

She swallowed and slammed the lid of the case down. 'If you won't go away, I will,' she whispered, and strode past him into the kitchen. But he caught her at the outer door, although, as she prepared to resist him, she discovered that in fact he was pushing her outside, and then she realised why.

He said abruptly, 'Come for a drive. You're right, this has gone on long enough. I'm not enjoying it either, so maybe we can hammer out some solution.'

'No!'

But she was no match for his strength and in the end he simply picked her up and placed her inside the Jaguar parked illegally against the kerb. Nor was he even breathing heavily when he said, 'Martha, dear, that's exactly the kind of scene that's fuelled this whole business out of all proportion.' But he did drive off with a vicious little squeal of tyres.

'If you didn't make me do things I don't want to do,' she hissed, but had to wipe crazy tears from her eyes, 'it wouldn't keep happening.'

'No? I've got the feeling things were never destined to be anything less than explosive between us,' he drawled. And he said no more as he threaded the big car expertly through the streets of London.

It was she who broke the silence at last as they left the city behind and he put on speed. 'Where are you taking me?'

'To a pub I know on the river. For lunch. I would appreciate it, seeing as I have no intention of seducing you, compromising you or making a fool of you, if you would refrain from making any kind of scene while we're there.'

'I wish *you'd* refrained last night,' she retorted, but with a rather tell-tale break in her voice that caused him to glance at her sharply. She shrugged, then said defiantly to cover any chink in her armour, 'I'm not dressed for much, in case you hadn't noticed.'

For a moment she thought it was a faintly bleak smile that played around his lips before he replied, 'Come off it, Martha. You must know you'd look good in a sack.'

She looked down at her faded, favourite jeans and plain blue blouse, and grimaced.

The pub was lovely, the sun was hot and they sat in the garden under a willow tree with the river slipping past not far away.

'One thing you have done,' Simon Macquarie said as he inspected a frosted bottle of wine he'd ordered with their lunch, 'is bring rather incredible summer weather with you.'

'I'm glad there's something I can do right,' Martha said. 'In your eyes, that is,' she added flatly.

'Yes, well, Yvette has made a startling claim,' he said slowly.

Martha put down her knife and fork. The fish she'd ordered was firm and white in a light golden batter and accompanied by a fresh salad. 'In what respect?'

He stared into her eyes for a long moment before his gaze drifted down to her breasts beneath the blue cotton.

'That you're not the rather sleazy person I took you for,' he said casually at last, withdrawing his gaze entirely and studying his steak contemplatively instead.

Martha breathed once, jerkily, then made herself eat a mouthful instead of flying into speech. 'So?' she said eventually. 'How did this come up anyway?'

'During her lurid accusations last night and this morning.' He smiled drily. 'She said, if you really want to know, "Why are you treating her like this? Why is she reacting this way? It doesn't make sense. She's such a good, sane, sensible girl."'

'At which, no doubt, you couldn't resist enlightening her,' Martha murmured, and picked up her wine glass, directing him a brief, very blue glance over its brim before she looked away.

'You're very contained all of a sudden, Martha.'

'I'm waiting with baited breath to hear if you were at all persuaded,' she said with irony.

'It's a little difficult for me to be so persuaded about you,' he answered with equal irony.

'That was three years ago. Did it never occur to you that things might not have been quite what they seemed?' she asked, and winced as her voice came out curiously husky.

'I told you—yes, it did. You denied it.'

'Well, I have to confess there's something about you, Simon Macquarie——' she tipped a hand '—that brings out the worst in me.'

He studied her narrowly for a long moment. 'So what are you trying to say, Martha?'

Here it is, she thought, almost like a blow to the solar plexus. The chance to square things—do I want to? Does he in any way deserve the truth? Can I ever explain what happened three years ago without...without giving away things I'd rather die than give away?

'I——' she said, and stopped as a voice said brightly behind them,

'Simon! Here you are. I tried to ring you when Dave and Miranda called and suggested lunch but there was no answer—what a coincidence!'

And Martha's gaze widened as she saw Simon Macquarie swear beneath his breath then stand up to greet the three people who came into view—including the owner of the voice, Sondra Grant.

If she got a shock to see who was with Simon, to Sondra's credit, she blinked twice then continued brightly, 'Why, if it isn't Martha Winters! I've really wanted to meet you, Martha—what a pity there isn't a photographer in sight! We could dispel all this nonsense about you and Simon in a flash, couldn't we?' And she laughed, displaying beautiful teeth, then turned to Simon to say, 'Darling, since you've not finished your lunch and we're *starving*, perhaps you could arrange another table?'

'Of course,' he said, and shook hands with the other couple. 'Dave, Miranda—meet Martha Winters. Martha, Dave and Miranda have just returned from their honeymoon in Australia as a matter of fact.'

Thank God for Australia, Martha was to think afterwards. Do you know how you saved the day for me?

Because indeed Dave and Miranda's enthusiasm and absolute delight at meeting an Australian who they could describe all the wonders they'd seen to took care of most awkward moments and soon set the conversation zinging along. They'd also, Martha realised, missed all the gossip and not apparently taken in, or decided discreetly to ignore, Sondra's opening remark to Martha. What did become apparent, however, was that Sondra had missed the Sunday papers.

Because she said, but not until the latter part of the lunch, 'So how was the Fashion Guild ball, darling? Another triumph for Yvette? What a nuisance I couldn't make it but it *was* Mama's birthday.'

'It was the usual,' Simon said as Martha moved awkwardly and nearly knocked over her wine glass. 'Unfortunately, Martha and I copped it again.'

'You two will just have to stop meeting like that,' Sondra said gaily, and changed the subject, but this time a little abruptly.

The party broke up not long afterwards. Martha made the return journey in the back seat of the Jaguar while Sondra acted as a perfectly charming hostess.

She was, Martha decided, amid her discomfort and the disbelief that this could be happening to her, not quite the bossy, brainy type Madame had made her out to be. She certainly held her own, often forceful opinions, and there was obviously a quick intelligence beneath her glossy, rather exotic looks and she was undoubtedly socially adept. Yet Martha couldn't help getting several other impressions throughout the afternoon: that Sondra Grant was an oddly down-to-earth person and that she wasn't altogether sure of Simon Macquarie and was treading carefully. Are they engaged or not? she found herself wondering. Sondra was not wearing a ring. As for Simon, there was nothing particularly lover-like in his manner towards the other girl, but they did do certain things as a couple.

Sondra had slid her arm through his as they'd left the pub, for example, and he hadn't rejected the move at all, and she'd slid into the front seat of the Jaguar automatically. She'd also chosen a cassette for the tape-player without consulting him and as if she was totally familiar with all his tapes, and they'd chatted about her parents for a few minutes as if Simon knew them well. Almost, the thought crossed Martha's mind as she'd listened, like a married couple... Which, of course, was a contradiction to Sondra not being sure of him.

So all in all it was an enormous relief when she saw familiar Chelsea roll past the windows, a relief which was to be replaced by acute consternation when Sondra turned to her as the car pulled up and said, 'Martha, it's been such fun meeting you. I'm giving a dinner party on Wednesday night—just a few friends, and Simon, of course!' She patted him playfully on the shoulder. 'I'd be delighted if you'd join us.'

Martha's first reaction was to think, Please don't let me be looking as horrified as I feel. 'Well, I...I...'

But Simon turned and his greeny grey eyes were entirely enigmatic as he murmured, 'Yes, do come, Martha. Why don't I pick you up? What time, Sondra?'

'About seven. Oh, I've had a brain wave! I'll invite Ricky. There's Yvette waving to us, Simon. Do you mind if we don't go in, darling? I thought we might just have a light meal and an early night, and, much as I love Yvette, it's a bit hard to get away from her sometimes...'

'You're staying?' Madame asked.

Martha breathed in several times. 'I'm...bemused,' she said at last.

'Well, I don't understand at all how Sondra got in on the act. You and Simon were supposed to be sorting out your differences today.'

Martha eyed Madame with some irony then explained what had happened. She also delivered the news of the dinner party.

Madame's eyebrows shot up. 'Silly girl!' she muttered. 'I told you she was brainy and bossy.'

'I don't quite see the connection,' Martha said slowly, 'but if you imagine for one moment that I intend to go to war with her over Simon Macquarie or something like that I'm not.'

'Would I dream anything like that?' Madame queried with an injured air.

'Yes,' Martha said tartly.

'But you will go?'

Martha's shoulders slumped. 'Believe it or not, I got outmanoeuvred. I don't know why; it doesn't happen to me often.'

'I believe it. I mean that it doesn't 'appen to you often,' Madame said hastily. 'Did you know I make the best omelettes in London?'

Martha blinked.

Madame shrugged.

'Are you offering—to make me an omelette?'

'I thought after the kind of day you've 'ad, on top of the kind of night you 'ad, a light supper and an early night might be nice. This is all,' Madame said sternly.

For some reason, not that it was entirely unknown to Martha, she had to laugh. But she said, 'Thank you. I would love an omelette.'

They had a slight dispute early Wednesday evening about what Martha chose to wear to Sondra Grant's dinner party. Madame arrived at the area door with a garment bag over her arm to find Martha already dressed, and determined to stay dressed in her own clothes.

'Well, it's fairly nice,' Madame pronounced of the longish blue linen skirt in panels and cream blouse with wide shoulders, full sleeves and tight cuffs, 'but thees is stunning!' She tapped the garment bag.

'No, Madame,' Martha said gently but firmly. 'I wouldn't say this is going to be pleasure exactly but it's not business.' And she ran her brush once more through her hair, which she was wearing long and loose, and slipped her narrow, high-arched feet into a pair of navy kid court shoes.

'You should never lose an opportunity to be stunning, Martha Winters,' Madame said repressively. 'You think I'm trying to turn this into an exercise in crass commercialism? I deny it! I simply want you to look your very best.'

'Pardon me,' a voice said from the doorway, 'but I can't see anything wrong with the way she looks.'

They both swung round to see Simon lounging in the area doorway looking amused.

Madame immediately heaved an exaggerated sigh. 'When a man has spoken, what can one do? Now you look after her tonight, Simon,' she added. 'No more sending her all set to fly back to Australia—it's not good for my nerves.'

'You're very quiet, Martha,' he said as they drove through the golden evening.

'We've only gone a few blocks,' she replied, but couldn't resist adding, 'Truth to tell I find this a bit incredible.'

They stopped at a traffic-light and as he changed gear she discovered herself watching his hand and feeling the kind of frisson she'd felt three years ago—which was like being slapped in the face, so she removed her gaze to the traffic-lights a little desperately.

'That Sondra should invite you to dinner?'

'Yes. And that you should second the invitation.'

'But then we had already decided to defuse the situation, hadn't we? You and I, I mean.'

'After you had the last laugh—did we? And do you mean to say that you and Sondra planned this together?'

He glanced at her then drove off smoothly. 'No. She took me by surprise too.'

'So——' Martha broke off and bit her lip.

He raised an eyebrow. 'Go on.'

'No, it doesn't matter.' She swallowed.

'She's a rather determined sort of person.'

'So I see.' But what she also saw was the faint smile that played across his lips before she withdrew her gaze and said a tinge wearily, 'Look, she can't have been *thrilled* by all this, and if you must know I would really like to say to her that none of it was my doing, but I can't without...without...'

'Putting me in?' he suggested wryly. 'I wonder why you hesitate to say it, let alone do it.'

'In the hope that we could all get out of this with the least harm done? No, don't say it,' she warned.

'What?'

'That you find that hard to believe of me. I know——'

'Why are you putting words in my mouth, Martha?'

She bit her lip in frustration. 'I'm not. It's what you've said or implied often enough.'

'My apologies. Go on.'

'I don't know what else there is to say... She's *your* fiancée after all.'

'Who told you that?'

'Madame.'

He grinned. 'I should have thought that by now you would have realised Yvette exaggerates sometimes.'

'So?'

'No, Martha,' he said deliberately. 'We are not engaged. What difference would you say that makes?'

'Not even unofficially?'

'Not even unofficially.'

'But...but...' Martha said disjointedly, then, 'You act like a couple.'

'Do we?'

'Yes, although——' No, don't say that, she warned herself.

'I await your words of wisdom.'

'Oh, *hell*,' she said through her teeth. 'What does it matter to me what you are? Just don't try to tell me she wouldn't give her eye-teeth to be engaged to you.'

'She hasn't told me that so far. I believe we're being very mature and adult about these things.'

'Look, are you having an affair with her or not? Because if you're not you can just turn round and take me home.'

'You said only moments ago that it didn't matter to you what Sondra and I were. So you'll have to explain this about-face——'

'Shut up,' Martha said fiercely, 'and listen. *I* thought what she had in mind tonight, because she struck me as a fairly practical sort of person, was a fence-mending exercise, and because I felt indirectly guilty—although God knows why I should—I was going to——'

'Fall all over Ricky Asquith-Font?' Simon Macquarie suggested placidly. 'I thought you might. Incidentally, here we are. St John's Wood. Now, Martha, just think what would happen if I had to go in there now and explain to everyone that you'd cried off—indeed run off—at the last moment?'

'I've changed my mind,' Martha said abruptly. 'I'll never feel guilty again if Sondra Grant doesn't get you to the altar. I'll rejoice for her instead!'

It was an elegant and accomplished dinner party.

Sondra served good food with the minimum of fuss, the wine flowed, her flat was discreetly luxurious and modern in décor and the company blended well. There were two other couples apart from Ricky, Dave and Miranda and an engaged couple, Linda and Michael.

Martha couldn't help but be aware that she was the object of some curiosity at first: Linda had it in her eyes and Miranda had obviously been filled in because she too at first looked a little nervous, but, in a display of almost social genius, Sondra made no explanations at all, made Martha apparently genuinely welcome and, with some help from Ricky, who was in bubbling good form, smoothed the first few awkward minutes with an expert hand. Then she kept it up all evening long, as well as indisputably but subtly laying absolute claim to Simon, leaving Martha to think that she'd make an outstanding wife, if one required a wife with social skills, and to wonder what was really going on in the other girl's mind.

But there were times, with Dave and Miranda still dazzled by their Australian honeymoon and with Ricky beside her and obviously particularly happy to be so, when it was a lively, enjoyable dinner party, and she was almost able to forget her awful feud with Simon Macquarie.

She was also instrumental in providing him with a couple of surprises during the evening—when she was lured into describing life on the sheep station she'd grown up on and how they'd used motorbikes to herd the sheep—she'd been able to ride a motorbike since she was twelve and sat on her first horse at the age of four, much to Ricky's delight. And when, at Dave's enthusiastic prompting, she'd recited Banjo Patterson's hilarious poem about a polo game between a country side and a team of city slickers, at the same time unwittingly revealing her love and knowledge of Australian folklore and poets such as A.B. Patterson and Henry Lawson. Both times his greeny gaze had rested on her enigmatically for the most part, but also slightly narrowed and probing—as if he was probing the mystery of why none of this had come to light three years ago.

Let him wonder, Martha found herself thinking tartly, still smarting over some of the things he'd said in the car. Let him jolly well wonder...

It came to an end about eleven o'clock and she tensed afresh as she wondered if he was going to insist on taking her home. Don't you dare! She tried to beam the message mentally. Don't do it to her, or me. But he didn't. When Ricky offered, assuring her that he had a car, not his bike, she accepted gratefully and no one made any demur.

In fact Simon put his arm around Sondra's shoulders as they bid their guests farewell and she looked up at him with her heart in her eyes for a brief moment, before reverting to her cheerful, practical self.

All that remained then for Martha was to deal with Ricky Asquith-Font as he drove almost agonisingly slowly home in his brand-new, bright red Porsche.

'You do like me, don't you, Martha?' he said not long after they set out.

Martha sighed inwardly. 'Yes, I do, Ricky. But I'm not—how can I put it?—going to get serious about you or any other man for that matter just yet.' And she grinned across at him to take the sting out of it.

'Because of Simon?'

'Not at all.' Her smile faded.

'Ah-ha.'

'What does that mean?'

'I don't know. I guess it means I'm confused. As well as a bit smitten.' He rolled his eyes at her.

She had to smile again. 'Actually I think you're sweet,' she murmured, 'and I'm happy to have you as a friend, but...' She stopped and shrugged.

'Talk about being damned with faint praise!' he said ruefully. 'I suppose the only saving grace is that you didn't say you'd like me for a brother.'

'Well, now you mention it——'

'Martha! Don't you dare,' he warned. 'There is absolutely nothing sisterly about what I feel for you.'

'Oh, Ricky, I'm sorry but...there it is,' she said a little awkwardly but with an underlying streak of firmness.

'Never mind. Why don't you come riding with me tomorrow morning—in the park? I keep a couple of hacks in town.'

'I don't think it's a very good idea—and I don't have any proper clothes. And definitely not tomorrow morning.'

But unfortunately he caught the faintly wistful note in her voice and said promptly, 'Leave it to me, Martha!' And he delivered her to her door untouched.

If Madame was bursting with curiosity over the next days, she hid it extraordinarily well. In fact she didn't refer to the dinner party at all, leaving Martha, who'd been prepared to fend her off, feeling as if she'd had the wind taken out of her sails. But it's all to the good, isn't it? she asked herself. It means that it's all dying down. Perhaps I can even begin to relax and try to put Simon Macquarie into some sort of perspective. Such as, for example? a traitorous inner voice enquired. Well...experience, she told it.

But several weeks later she had to change her mind.

Good as his word, Ricky appeared on her doorstep one evening bearing a pair of jodhpurs, riding boots and a hard hat. They belonged to one of his sisters, he said, of which he had five. She was more than happy to lend them to Martha and would be joining them the next morning for a ride along Rotten Row.

Thus it was that she got into the pattern of riding with Ricky and his sister two or three times a week, and, for the first time since coming to London, made a friend of the female sex. Ricky's sister Annabel was twenty-six, a comely redhead with a quick wit and none of her brother's passion for motorbikes but was mad about horses. She also had no airs and graces despite being Lady Annabel. They clicked almost immediately, a bit to Ricky's chagrin, had lunch a couple of times, went to a concert in the Albert Hall once and on a shopping spree.

'It's good,' Madame pronounced when she surprised them one evening eating toasted cheese in the basement flat and giggling like a couple of girls at a television comedy. 'Martha gets a bit uptight sometimes; she needs a friend.'

Martha grimaced but said nothing, possibly because it was true. Yet it was almost directly through Annabel that she ran into Simon again—with such disastrous consequences . . .

'Come to the polo with me,' Annabel said one day. 'There's this divine Australian I've got my eye on but I need a bit of moral support. There'll probably be a bit of a bash after the matches so bring a gladrag to throw on just in case.'

'Where?'

'Wherever,' Annabel said with a mischievous look, then relented. 'They're playing at the stately home of a friend of mine; it's some sort of charity gala thing—we're welcome to stay the night if we want to.'

Martha hesitated but Annabel persisted and she finally gave in—and was glad she had on the day. It was a beautiful weekend after a showery, overcast week; the field and surrounding countryside smelt tantalisingly of wet earth but were a brilliant green beneath a cloudless blue sky. There were horses everywhere, beautiful game little polo ponies that made Martha catch her breath.

It wasn't until later in the afternoon that she saw Simon Macquarie ride out on to the field. Fortunately Annabel was chatting to friends—they were sitting in the stand—and didn't notice Martha tense. And by the time she turned back the first chukka was in progress and Martha had herself under control and was able to parry her new friend's slight look of concern with a shrug.

'I should have thought of that,' Annabel said slowly. 'He doesn't play much now, which is a pity because he used to be brilliant.'

'It doesn't matter. It was all a crazy press beat-up anyway,' Martha said. 'We met in Australia years ago and ... didn't like one another. He was the last person in the world I expected to run into and I'm sure the same held good for him. Oh, look, your divine Aussie is in the same team!'

And that, quite effectively, took Annabel's mind off Simon Macquarie, although the same couldn't be said for Martha.

In fact it was a curious form of torture to watch his expert horsemanship, his lithe grace in the saddle, his strength and his occasional wry look when he mistimed a shot. It was also peculiarly difficult from then on not to act as if she would give heaven and earth to be elsewhere. When she did finally suggest to Annabel that she'd make her own way back to London because she'd decided to give the bash a miss, she was smartly disabused of the idea.

'Apart from anything else, Martha Winters, you're here to give me *Australian* moral support. Mind you, though, you're so gorgeous I'm probably out of my mind. But, be that as it may, you can't spend your life running away from Simon.'

'Annabel, I——'

'Trust me, Martha!'

Which was how it came about that later, when she was wearing a short-skirted sleeveless yellow linen dress and drinking champagne in the huge marquee beneath a slowly darkening sky, she—inevitably, she thought wearily, despite the lively throng—ran into him.

'Hello, Martha,' he said quietly, when they both turned to find they'd been standing back to back. He was still in his white breeches and boots with a tweed jacket over his shirt, and his gaze skimmed the short dress and her bare golden legs and arms briefly before returning to hers.

She said, 'Hello, Simon,' equally quietly, and could think of not another word to say as the world seemed to tilt a little.

'Are you here on your own?'

'No.' She explained and was at the same time intensely relieved to find that things had come back to normal, including her command of her tongue. 'I didn't realise you played polo,' she finished, and smiled faintly.

'Or you wouldn't have come?'

'No,' she said barely audibly.

His eyes glinted. 'But there are a lot of things we didn't realise about each other, aren't there, Martha?'

'Perhaps,' she conceded, 'but of course that's all water under the bridge now—— Would you excuse me? I see Annabel over there—— Oh!'

'Yes, she's coming this way and waving at you to stay put,' he murmured. 'So you may have to grin and bear my company for a bit longer. I see she also has a compatriot of yours in tow. How's Ricky?'

'Fine,' Martha said stiffly.

'You've made quite a hit with the Asquith-Fonts.'

Martha stared down at the golden bubbles in her glass and was horrified to find herself suddenly blinking away ridiculous tears. 'Well,' she said huskily, her head still bent, 'I wouldn't put it quite like that.'

'Martha—look at me,' he commanded softly.

It was with a supreme effort that she banished the tears and looked up at last. 'Why? So you can pin me to a cloth like a butterfly and torment the life out of me? Do note, incidentally, that I'm doing my best not to make a scene, despite all this provocation.' And she managed to smile mechanically up at him.

His eyes narrowed and she thought he'd guessed about the tears she'd battled with—perhaps, even, she thought with fresh horror, the sheen of them was still there for all to see.

'I——' She started to say something, anything, but he overrode her abruptly.

'Why? Don't you *remember* playing a hard-hearted, common little tart for all you were worth, Martha?' he said, and added, with a lethal sort of gentleness that cut like ice, 'If you were to show me the real Martha Winters, we might be able to finish this once and for all.'

'Martha!' It was Annabel, dragging her divine Australian behind her, finally reaching them. 'Hello, Simon!' she said brightly, and reached up to peck him on the cheek. 'Good to see you two chatting—Martha, meet Paul. He comes from a place called Scone in New South Wales—and don't you dare fall for her, Paul!' she ordered with a cheeky grin and a swish of her long red hair. '*I* saw you first! Martha,' she continued, 'we thought of going to a place near by for a bite to eat— this is becoming a real bash,' she added with a grimace.

'Oh, I...' Martha hesitated as she contemplated playing gooseberry, and knew suddenly that she just didn't have the energy or whatever it required. 'I really think I'll go home, Annabel,' she said, then stopped again frustratedly as she saw Annabel take a determined breath and at the same time wondered a little wildly how she would get home at this time of night.

'Martha—but how?' Annabel demanded. 'Now don't——'

'It so happens I'm going back to London tonight,' Simon Macquarie said smoothly.

CHAPTER FOUR

'WHAT about your horses?' Martha said tensely, back in the Jaguar again.

'I haven't got any these days. I've given up polo to all intents and purposes. They were——' he slid an arm along the back of the seat and turned to watch through the rear window as he reversed the car '—borrowed ones I was riding today.'

'Oh.'

'Yes. Any more objections?' he said gravely as he turned back and set the car going forward. 'Or is it a case of the lady protesting just a little too much?' he added idly as they bounced a bit over the rutted track. 'You are here after all, and I didn't precisely kidnap you.'

Martha's nostrils flared but she said flatly, 'I didn't relish playing companion to those two——'

'Afraid he might fall for you—and break up your beautiful new friendship? I don't suppose he has an earldom around the corner.'

Martha sat back and forced herself to relax. 'It'll be interesting to see just how insulting you can be, Simon. I suppose——' she glanced at her watch '—I've got about an hour and a half to find out.'

'That's my Martha,' he murmured with a smile twisting his lips.

She said nothing as they gained the road, and nothing for a good ten minutes afterwards as the big car ate up the miles. In fact as the silent miles progressed she laid her head back, but although she felt bone-weary her eyes refused to close on her rather torturous thoughts . . .

It was he who said at last, 'Why don't you put some music on?'

'No—that's Sondra's job,' she answered, almost without thinking.

'Sondra's not here.'

'Her presence is,' she replied barely audibly, and turned her head on the squab to look out of the side-window, away from him.

He said nothing but she heard the tape-box click open, some more clicks and then Dvořák filled the car, the *New World Symphony* and the almost unbearably haunting strains of the Negro spiritual 'Going Home' that the composer had woven into his music. It had, quite suddenly, a curiously devastating effect on her...

She sat up abruptly and put her hands to her face as silent tears started to stream down her cheeks.

'Martha?'

He said her name once and then stopped the tape and pulled the car off the road. But he didn't attempt to touch her as the storm of tears subsided and he switched on the overhead light as she groped in her purse for a hanky, saying hoarsely at the same time, 'Sorry. That was stupid of me. We can go on now.'

'I don't think we can go on at all—not like this.'

She took a breath, blew her nose then said in that same harsh voice, 'All right. What do you want—a confession? Here goes: I was only nineteen, I was furious with the world at large and with——'

'Furious?'

She bit her lip and explained briefly about her parents' futile fight against a deadly drought and having to leave their property with almost nothing.

'So,' he said quietly. 'I wondered about that when you were describing the place at Sondra's party the other night. Go on—you were furious with the world in general and with...?'

'And with men who tried to fondle me in particular,' Martha said acidly. 'And when you mistook me for a tramp or a tart I thought——' she shrugged '—so be it. But at the same time I was a bit smitten,' she said precisely and with a defiant glance, although she winced as soon as the words left her mouth, thinking of Ricky among other things. 'However much I tried to tell myself I wasn't,' she went on bleakly after a moment, then stopped again, with a sigh this time.

'So you hated me for my mistake, which, incidentally, looked for all the world——'

'Yes, well,' Martha said drily, recovering herself. 'I was just about to drive my heel into his shoe when you—collared me.'

There was a moment's dead silence then Simon Macquarie started to laugh softly. 'What about Vinny?' he said at last, still smiling.

'Vinny?' She looked perplexed.

'Your Latin lover who arrived the night we...' He gestured wryly.

'Oh, *Vinny*!' Martha grimaced and explained, finishing, 'He leapt back ten paces every time I met him after that.'

'I might have known,' Simon said. 'The trouble was I didn't know you then.'

'Nor do you know me now,' she said coolly.

'I...see,' he said slowly. 'Are you trying to tell me you got over being a bit smitten?'

'I've concluded over the last three years that it was one of those spurious physical attractions that nineteen-year-old girls are rather renowned for suffering, especially in regard to older, more sophisticated men.'

'Martha,' he mocked, 'that sounds incredibly pompous!'

She turned like a flash, her drenched blue eyes glittering with anger, her whole body as taut as a wound-up spring beneath the yellow linen, and she was quite uncaring of the tear and mascara stains on her face as she hissed, 'Go to hell, Simon Macquarie! That's *exactly* how it happened and that's all there is to it.'

'Well, unfortunately I have to dispute that,' he said, his mouth suddenly grim. 'Because I'll tell you what also happened: we never did get enough of each other, and while we're constantly being thrown into each other's company things will continue to explode between us— until we do.'

Martha gasped and went rigid but he went on, with that slightly grim set to his mouth suddenly relaxed and his eyes full of amused irony, 'I did think, my dear, that if you knew it was something mutual you might see it in a better light.'

'Better light?' she whispered, then, 'Mutual...? How *dare* you——?'

'Oh, come on, Martha,' he said with a rough edge of impatience. 'We both know damn well that once I started to kiss you we would—it would please you as much as it would me; it certainly used to.'

Martha took a huge breath to stop herself trembling. 'And what about the years in between?' she said. 'I haven't explained away *them* as yet.'

He said nothing for a moment and then, with that narrowed, penetrating look she'd come to fear and detest, he said drily, 'Look, you're all grown-up now, I would imagine, and what's been has been—it's your affair in other words. Just as my affairs are mine.'

'Sondra—in other words?' she parodied.

'I've told you about Sondra—there's nothing binding between us.'

'So will you come and go between us, sort of thing, Simon? Or have you got enough of Sondra and I'm a fresh field, for want of better words?'

The silence was taut and intense between them for about two minutes. Then he said quite gently but with deadly accuracy, 'Do you think we'd even be saying these things if we didn't want each other, Martha? I think not.'

A faint tinge of colour came to her pale cheeks. But she said bravely, 'I think I'm telling you exactly why it's not on, Simon.'

'And I think you're telling me your pride has never recovered, Martha.'

This was so true, but at the same time such a small part of the truth that she paled again and closed her eyes, and therefore was quite unprepared when he said, almost idly, 'Well, be that as it may, we could always put one thing to the test.'

Her lashes flickered up. 'What?'

'This.' And he leant over, flicked the tape out, put another in, and when some lovely lilting Brahms was playing softly he said, 'Whatever else you might like to think of me, I didn't intend to make you feel homesick and bereft, so perhaps I can remedy that—at least. Because I have to admire you and the way you've taken on the world, however you've done it...' And while she stared at him, mesmerised, he drew her into his arms.

'Perhaps we could put this down as a salute between two slightly battle-scarred contenders,' he said as he touched her mouth with one finger. 'Would that suit you, Martha?'

But before she had a chance to reply he lowered his head and was kissing her and running his fingers through her hair.

*　*　*

It was a pale, overcast dawn that filtered through her bedroom curtains and gradually illuminated the ceiling that she'd been staring at blindly and despairingly for half the night. Despairingly because it had been the same old magic, impossible to resist; impossible not to respond to Simon Macquarie, not to shiver with expectation as those long, strong fingers had stroked her skin and his mouth had claimed hers, lightly at first, then deeper and deeper ... So that when they'd finally drawn apart she'd been breathing like a long-distance runner— and so, although to a lesser extent, had he.

But he'd said nothing, although the query in his eyes had been unmistakable.

Yet rationality had started to surface as her breathing had steadied—rationality and the kind of despair that had become such a close companion—and her pulse-rate had lowered and she'd realised what she'd done: given herself in all but the final way to a man who was just as likely to leave her one day as he'd done before, a man who used the most deadly weapons against her. She'd given herself to the enemy in other words, and for the second time ...

So, as it had all flooded through her, she'd lowered her eyes deliberately against that query, and turned away. And after a moment he'd started the engine and driven the rest of the way home in silence. Nor had he made any attempt to stop her as she'd slipped from the car outside Madame's house. He'd simply driven off.

'You're not well?'

'I'm fine, Madame,' Martha said later that morning.

'You don't look it! You have shadows under your eyes, you have no zip, no zest.'

'Perhaps that's because I'm not sure whether I'm meant to be an urchin, an orphan or a tramp!' Martha said with a suddenly blazing look. 'I'm five feet ten, I'm no Twiggy and these baggy, raggedy kind of things just don't suit me—there is difference between looking like a tomboy and a waif!'

Madame drew herself up. 'You dare to tell me my sportswear is baggy and raggedy?'

'No,' Martha said exasperatedly. 'I——'

'But you just said——'

'I said—what I meant was,' Martha amended, 'there's a look and a face and figure to go with this kind of gear and I don't think it's me!'

'You're right.'

'I beg your pardon?' Martha's eyes widened.

Madame threw up her hands. 'I said you're *right*, because with a figure like yours it's a crime to cover it up in bagginess. What more do you want me to do—get on my 'ands and grovel?' And she eyed her in-house model aggressively.

Martha put a hand to her brow and had to smile. 'Sorry—no, of course not. What will you do?'

'Throw the baggy ones away. Which means we 'ave finished shooting the *prêt-à-porter* so you can take a break. Go to Scotland for a week, Martha. London is too 'ot but Scotland will bring the roses back to your cheeks. I know, I lived there once,' she finished ruefully.

Martha stared at her a bit dazedly but when she found her voice it was to say, 'Thank you but the last place on earth I would go to is Scotland.'

'He won't be there; he's in Bordeaux.'

'Who?'

'Who do you think, Martha?' Madame said dangerously. 'Simon!'

'How...rather why...do you think it's necessary to tell me that?'

Madame shrugged. 'He told me so 'imself—not to tell you exactly.' She grimaced and added, 'When he dropped your bag off this morning.'

Martha bit her lip and sat down. She'd entirely forgotten the bag of clothes that had been transferred from Annabel's car to the Jaguar. 'OK,' she said wearily. 'What else did he say?'

'Nothing! But you see, I can tell from the tone of 'is voice when he says nothing, and from the look of you, Miss Martha, that there 'ave been goings-on again. Only this time I think you make 'im really mad,' she added slyly. 'Did you...is it too much to 'ope that you did it in private?'

'No,' Martha said, but even to her own ears her voice had a hollow ring to it.

'I think that was wise.'

'There was nothing wise about it at all as it happened.'

'Ah.'

'Yes, well—but why Scotland?' Martha said drily and still with a trace of suspicion in her voice.

'You could do me a good turn at the same time.'

Martha raised an eyebrow.

'Tartan,' Madame said succinctly.

'Tartan?'

'Yes, that stuff the Scots tend to wear a lot. I'm convinced it will be big next season so I've prepared a couple of outfits in advance and I'd like some preliminary pics. With Edinburgh Castle in the background.'

'I see.'

'It would take one, at the most two days of your week, and take care of your travelling expenses. Thus,' Madame said, 'for the rest of your time you could hire a leetle car and go where the whim took you. In spite of the weather Scotland is very beautiful.'

It so happened, Martha mused, that despite her tragic association with a Scot she had always longed to see Scotland. Had it even heightened since meeting Simon Macquarie? she wondered, but found that too painful to contemplate for long...

'You did say you wanted to travel,' Madame murmured.

'But you won't be there?'

'Alas, no. I will be in Paris but I know I could rely on you to get things right.'

Martha grimaced. 'Who's the photographer?'

Madame mentioned a name and said, 'I don't know why but you come up better for him than anyone else. And who knows? In my tartan, you could end up on the cover of *Vogue*.'

Martha smiled suddenly. 'Why do I feel like a donkey?'

'Donkey?' Madame blinked.

'Being coaxed with a whole bunch of carrots... It doesn't matter, I'll go. As a matter of fact I've always wanted to see the Hebrides and Skye et cetera.'

'Good girl. Don't forget the Inner Hebrides—Arran, Iona and particulary Mull. It's truly beautiful.'

Which was how Martha came to spend two days being photographed on the battlements of Edinburgh Castle. When the photographer finally pronounced himself satisfied, with a sigh of relief she took the little car she'd hired and set off to explore Scotland—and promptly fell in love with it—rain or shine.

On the lovely island of Mull the sun shone brilliantly for her last couple of days. From Mull she explored Iona, where she felt a kind of wonder, possibly associated with being born in the Antipodes and having spent all her life reading about the British Isles and now actually being in the Hebrides, and standing on Macbeth's probable burial place. There was also a quality of light about the birthplace of Christianity in this part of the world that was unusually beautiful, although she discovered from the pamphlets she had that many and much more famous people than she had been struck by this, including Keats.

But she was in an unusually mellow mood as she drove back from the ferry at Fionnphort on Mull, along the shores of Loch Scridain towards her modest bed-and-breakfast lodging at Craignure, still thinking of Saint Columba and all the ringed Celtic crosses on Iona—when she found the road barred by some weird and woolly Highland cattle. So she stopped and watched them peacefully—there was no traffic on the road; all the ferry traffic had passed her—only to be unpleasantly jolted after about ten minutes by someone tooting a horn behind her.

What she least expected when she turned round was a very familiar dark blue Jaguar... It can't be, she thought, with her heart suddenly beating like a drum. No! But it was...

For an equally familiar tall figure stepped out of the Jaguar, came up to her window, started to say pleasantly enough that he was in a bit of a hurry, unfortunately, then stopped short as their gazes clashed.

That was when Simon Macquarie went on, not at all pleasantly, 'Bloody hell! If this is Yvette's doing I'll strangle her. Or is it?'

For a moment Martha's tongue seemed to cleave to the roof of her mouth then she said disjointedly but hotly, 'She said...she *told* me you were in Bordeaux.'

'She knew damn well I *wasn't*!'

Martha's mouth fell open. 'But...but...' she stammered. 'Do you mean you live here—on Mull?'

'Yes,' he said shortly. 'Well, the family home is here and I always spend a couple of weeks up here at this time of the year,' he added impatiently.

'I still don't see...she did recommend Mull——'

'I'll bet she did,' he said sardonically, 'since she knew it was exactly where I'd be.'

'But she couldn't have known we'd bump into each other like this!'

'Yvette,' he said coldly, 'is a conniving, extremely unprincipled woman at times. She's also a great taker of chances—if we hadn't met like this, she would have shrugged in a very French way and looked around for some other way of achieving this.'

Martha took a breath, blinked a couple of times and said with restrained anger, 'She's achieved nothing so far and if you'd be so good as to clear the road for me I'll drive on—or you can drive on first if you like and that'll be that.' And so saying she started up the car.

'Martha——'

'Don't "Martha" me, Simon Macquarie,' she said through her teeth, and revved the engine before putting it into gear—with disastrous consequences. One of the Highland cattle got a fright, bounded towards her briefly but just long enough to make her swerve wildly before it plunged off the side of the road, and the car too, in a series of leaps, went off the road before stalling.

Martha swore beneath her breath. She was in no way mollified at catching sight of her tormentor standing in the middle of the road with a faint smile on his face and his hands shoved into his pockets, and she started up again, determined to drive off and leave him standing there—only to discover she was bogged in a deep patch of mud.

She got out, slammed the door, but before she could launch into speech he said mildly, 'It's never wise to act in a temper, Martha. You're well and truly bogged.'

'And I'm well and truly—what the hell am I going to do?'

'You could ask me to help you,' he suggested gravely. She bit her lip and he laughed and murmured, 'Your expression almost defies description, but we shouldn't stand around chatting for too long—it's going to rain.'

Martha glanced upwards at the heavy black clouds she'd not noticed—all set to further wreck her lovely golden day. 'If you wouldn't mind, I'd be grateful,' she said stiffly.

'I wonder... Never mind,' he drawled, and turned back to the Jaguar.

It took half an hour to get the car out of the mud, during which the heavens opened and they both got soaked as well as mud-splattered; then it wouldn't start.

'Please—don't do this to me,' Martha muttered, and got out again to look under the bonnet.

'What are you doing?'

'Well, I can't sit here all night.'

'Of course you can't!' Simon said irritably. 'I'll put the tow-rope back on.'

'You mean you'll tow me back to Craignure?'

'Not bloody likely,' he replied. 'It's miles. I'll tow you home.'

'Well, I think I'd rather try to fix it; I know something about mechanics even if you don't,' she said pointedly.

'You——' he paused as they glared at each other with water dripping off their faces, the rain hammering down '—will get into that car and do as you're told, Martha

Winters. I'm soaked, I'm tired and I'm fed up to the back teeth. Now, do I have to make you? Because I can tell you, right at this moment it would give me a lot of pleasure.'

Martha stood in a stone-flagged foyer and a puddle started to form around her feet as a small, elderly, white-haired lady clucked over her.

'This is Martha, Grace,' Simon Macquarie introduced her. 'She's staying the night. Put her in the yellow bedroom, please. Any calls?'

Grace reeled off several names then turned back to Martha. 'You poor wee thing! But a nice hot bath will make you feel a whole lot better and I've got a plump duck roasting in the oven. Now come along before you catch your death.'

I might have known, Martha thought an hour or so later as she brushed her hair at the window of the yellow bedroom, that the family home would be like this.

It had stopped raining, but although it was still overcast there was enough light to see a wonderful view of the loch and a glorious azalea- and rhododendron-filled garden stretching down to its edge, as well as a daisy- and clover-studded meadow going up to the road, which was lined with huge trees. The house itself was two-storeyed and substantial, white with a green trim and plenty of chimneys, and evoked the phrase 'a minor manor-house'. It was also filled with beautiful furniture, drapes and carpets, paintings, porcelain, crystal and silver. And the yellow bedroom had a double four poster bed with yellow silk drapes that matched the wallpaper, all sorts of interesting knicknacks—were you in the frame of mind to be interested in such things—and an *en-suite* bathroom that was modern and luxurious.

Yes, she thought, looking down and turning the brush over and over in her hands, I should have known. I should also have known Yvette was up to something. I wonder if even she realised how wildly successful her machinations could be?

She lifted her head at a soft knock on the door. It was Grace.

'Oh, my, you do look nice,' she said.

Martha looked ruefully down at her slim ivory trousers and camellia blouse. 'It's nothing special.'

'Then it must be you. Simon asked me to tell you that dinner is nearly ready and would you join him for a drink now?'

'I...yes. Thank you. Uh, is there anyone else staying—in the house?' she asked awkwardly.

'Not a soul,' Grace said seriously but closed one eye in a mischievous little wink.

Leaving Martha to think, That's all I need.

'What would you like?'

'A dry sherry, thank you. Your house is lovely,' Martha added, and accepted her drink without looking into Simon Macquarie's eyes. She'd seen, on arriving in the drawing-room with its bow window overlooking the garden and loch, that he was showered and changed into light trousers and a dark green shirt.

'Thank *you*,' he murmured. 'Cheers.'

'Yes, cheers.' She sipped her sherry and wandered over to the window.

'Well, what are we going to talk about, Martha?'

She tensed and refused to look around. 'I don't know—you choose.'

'We could always discuss Yvette and why she has this obsession about fixing me up with you—or vice versa.'

That did make Martha turn and level a cool, dark blue look at him. 'I have no idea. Could it just be a burning desire to see you married off?'

He smiled. 'Do sit down. I can't think why if she has such a desire. I'm not doing anyone any harm by maintaining my unwedded state.'

'You are growing older, however.'

'You're right, it's probably that,' he said wryly and with an entirely unoffended, wicked little glint in his eyes. 'What about you?' he asked politely.

'If you must know, she feels a bit maternal about me sometimes. When she's not screaming at me and telling me I look like a sack of potatoes, that is.'

He looked genuinely surprised for a moment then he said slowly, 'I guess that's about the only other thing that makes sense of it. Why you, though?'

'I remind her of herself at the same age.' Martha grimaced. 'Apparently she was an angry young woman.'

He laughed softly. 'I see. Well, then, how are we going to rid her of this obsession?'

But Grace put her head around the door then to say that she'd served the soup. So they took their glasses into a charming conservatory that looked like an addition to the house and had a genuine grape-vine growing across the roof. The table was set for two and there was a slender yellow candle in a silver holder, reflecting its golden light against the glass.

'This is lovely,' Martha said a shade desperately as she unfurled her napkin and waited, wincing, for an ironic reply.

But Simon looked around and said, 'It was my mother's idea. She was responsible for the gardens too— I mean they've been here for ages but she reclaimed it all from the wilderness it had become.'

Martha drank some soup. 'Tell me some more about your mother.'

The irony did come through then but only briefly as he said, 'A nice, safe subject—well, perhaps you're right. She was one of the nicest people I knew.'

'I'm sorry,' Martha murmured. 'What about your father?'

'Well, I think he was one of the biggest bastards I ever knew,' Simon said meditatively. 'He certainly made her life hell.'

Martha stared at him, her spoon poised, her eyes wide. 'Why?'

'Why do men make women's life hell? You probably have to get behind the bedroom door to discover that, but in general he was a stiff, selfish kind of man; he was intensely correct and full of his own consequence—and he probably suffered considerable loss of ego because he wasn't the best businessman in the world. Whereas she was vague, sweet, funny sometimes, had no sense of consequence at all, although when it came to whom had the more impressive lineage, to put it diplomatically, she came from a much older family. She...' he paused and stared into the candle-flame '...year by year became diminished in spirit. I sometimes even think she was happy to almost fade away in the end.'

'That's terribly sad,' Martha said huskily. 'Why didn't she leave him?'

'Because he probably sapped all the resistance out of her. You may find that hard to believe.' He brought his gaze back to rest on her face at last and half smiled. 'An angry young woman like you, quote unquote. But we're not all made the same.'

'No, of course not,' Martha said quietly. 'Does it mean you're a bit cynical about the institution of marriage, though?'

He took his time about answering as he surveyed her a little narrowly. Then he said only, 'Perhaps.'

'You shouldn't be. You just said yourself we're not all the same.'

'Thank you for your concern,' he replied drily. 'Unless you're offering yourself for the position?'

Martha looked away with a set mouth and angry eyes. 'You're... you never give up do you?'

'Ah, well,' he drawled, 'that could be because I find myself in the position of wanting you, Martha, more than I've wanted any woman for some time.'

'Now how's tha' for a duck?' Grace said triumphantly a second later as she swept round the door bearing the golden, steaming bird aloft on a silver platter.

CHAPTER FIVE

'WHAT am I going to do?' Martha said barely audibly as she stared helplessly at her quarter-eaten meal. For not only had Grace provided roast duck and cherries but roast potatoes, cauliflower *au gratin*, roast pumpkin and green beans, and all this on top of pumpkin and leek soup. At the best of times it would have been a test of her appetite, and this was not the best of times at all. In fact after his pronouncement, after the flurry of carving and being served, when Grace had finally departed, there'd been a deadly little lull.

'Have I taken your appetite away, Martha?' Simon asked drily.

'Yes. No...I mean...' But she couldn't go on.

'Look, don't rush it. Relax—and have some wine.'

She took a trembling breath and reached for her wine glass.

'There's something I can't quite fathom about all this,' he said slowly, and watched her carefully over the rim of his own glass. He too had laid down his knife and fork. 'You did, by your own admission, set out to seriously mislead me three years ago. You also told me you'd put certain things down to an adolescent crush. Which is why I find it a little difficult to understand your pride taking *such* a hammering. If anything, what I said just now should have brought you quite some gratification.'

'Then you don't begin to know me at all,' she retorted. 'I told you that once before.'

94

He picked up his knife and fork and started to eat again, then said meditatively, 'OK—let's take this from another angle. There is obviously a lot we don't know about each other. I don't, for example, know how things have been for you in the intervening three years. Whether you've been let down in love, ill-treated or whatever it takes to induce cynicism in women. Why don't you tell me about that?'

Martha started reluctantly to eat—mainly as an exercise to disguise the turbulence of her thoughts. But finally she said, 'It's a little difficult to bare or share your past with a man who only a few hours ago expressed such disgust at seeing you again.'

'Martha,' he said softly, 'when you kiss a man the way you did a couple of weeks ago, and then walk away from him the way you did, I can assure you that most men would react with a certain degree of disgust.'

'Ah, but two can play at that game,' Martha said with a degree of wryness that made her proud. 'Even while you thought I was a tart or a tramp you came back for more, until you too walked away, and a whole lot further.'

He raised an ironic eyebrow at her. 'But I did draw the line at going to bed with you,' he murmured. And their gazes locked, his flecked with green and something she couldn't fathom, hers, despite herself and although she didn't know it, curiously wary. Then he added with soft mockery, 'I did do that. Are we not going round and round in useless circles, Martha?'

She was never sure afterwards what it was that made her come to a decision. It happened almost instinctively, as if she could no longer live a lie... She said, 'You're right. The thing is, I'd not been to bed with anyone before I met you—and the same still applies.' She paused, unsure of how to go on, and had the doubtful satisfaction of seeing his fingers tighten round the stem of his wine glass. She shrugged. 'I suppose by way of that being a rationale for all that's happened between us—having got to the grand old age of twenty-two untouched or whatever—I'm not about to throw it away on a man who a: walked away from me once, b: is involved with another woman and c: is just as likely to walk away from me again. There you have it in a nutshell, Simon. Of course, whether you believe me or not remains to be seen.' And she grimaced, pushed her plate away then raised defiant blue eyes to his.

'So,' he said, with an unusual expression in his eyes as his gaze rested on her breasts beneath the camellia blouse. 'I sometimes suspected that.'

Shock gripped her and her lips parted incredulously. 'Y-you...knew?' she stammered.

'No, I didn't,' he said drily, lifting his eyes to hers at last.

'But what made you suspect?'

He smiled briefly. 'There were some things you weren't terribly practised at. Some sensations that seemed to surprise you.'

'So I was...gauche as well as...' She stopped and bit her lip.

'As well as trying to convince me you weren't at the same time as never failing to let me know you didn't like me? In fact, Martha, you were astonishingly beautiful even when you were trying to be a tramp. Beautiful and full of life and fire. It was a heady combination,' he reflected. 'But I don't make a habit of deflowering virgins—not that I expected you to remain one for long if that's what you were, certainly not three years long. Why?' he said simply.

The yellow candle flamed suddenly and Martha looked up apprehensively, expecting Grace to descend on them again, but it was only a light breeze coming in through the window. Not that I couldn't do with a timely interruption, she thought.

'Let's take one thing at a time,' she said a little dazedly. 'You say you suspected that about me then but didn't consider it a possibility when we met again?'

His lips twisted. 'Don't forget I have to deal with all the misinformation you feed me, Martha,' he mocked. 'Nor did I say that exactly, but yes, I guess I assumed it had happened. You were so much more poised for one thing, for the most part.' His eyes glinted. 'You were absolutely stunning and you had been . . .' He paused as if he was choosing his words with care. 'Well, when I looked back at what had happened between us——'

'You couldn't believe the cherry hadn't fallen,' she said, and wondered if her voice had ever sounded bleaker.

'I'm not infallible, Martha,' he said with sudden rough impatience. 'Are you going to tell me why or not?'

She gathered every ounce of hard-won composure she possessed. 'I think it was quite simple—a lack of the right man. Well, two things, perhaps,' she amended. 'It wasn't easy to get to this.' She glanced down briefly at her clothes and then made a curiously eloquent little gesture that took in even her being in that part of the world and everything else she'd achieved. 'It certainly took a lot of time and hard work and I suppose I was determined not to be distracted until I'd made it.'

'So it wasn't at all because you couldn't forget what it was like in my arms—when you were in someone else's?'

She thought for a long moment before she replied steadily, 'What wasn't easy to forget was being made—or rather having made a fool of oneself.'

'You don't think that's evading the question?' he murmured, his eyes suddenly raking her face and her figure again.

Her hands trembled so she put them out of sight beneath the table. 'That's all I'm going to...that's all there is to say, Simon.'

'There is something I can say, though: I'm no longer involved with Sondra.'

Martha breathed jerkily. 'Why?'

He smiled but it didn't reach his eyes. 'Why do you think? I'm not, contrary to all your expectations, a two-woman man.'

'I...but...no, please tell me,' she whispered.

'Because you feel responsible? You are,' he said abruptly. 'That doesn't mean to say it's your fault.'

Martha flinched. 'It's a little hard to tell the difference.'

'Does it really worry you?'

'Yes!' She put the back of her hand to her mouth.

He pushed his own plate away and studied the contents of his wine glass thoughtfully. 'Sondra has a lot of wonderful qualities,' he said at last. 'Organisational qualities, social skills and so on, but there simply isn't the spark—that exists between you and I, for example. And I realised,' he went on as her eyes flew to his, 'that the rest of our lives would run smoothly and to a well-ordered pattern, and that it simply wasn't enough. In fact you've done her a favour, Martha, although what you've done for me remains to be seen.'

I sensed something like that, she thought. Or was it wishful thinking? Oh God, what do I do now? 'Do you mean whether we can turn that spark into anything more?' she hazarded. 'You said to me once that you thought things would always be explosive between us.'

'I haven't had the opportunity to prove or disprove that,' he said wryly.

Martha stood up abruptly. 'I can't eat any more. I'd like to go to bed, please.'

He stood up as well but treacherously rang the little silver bell. Martha's shoulders slumped as Grace responded almost immediately and she sat down again and murmured her apologies.

'That's all right!' Grace said brightly but glanced at Simon.

'If you wouldn't mind serving coffee in the drawing-room, Grace,' he murmured. 'I'm afraid Miss Winter's had a rather trying day.'

Grace clucked. 'Poor wee thing—now you just go and relax and I'll bring coffee then I'll be gone as soon as I've cleared away.'

'She doesn't live here?' Martha said some ten minutes later over a cup of coffee and a plate of macaroons in the drawing-room.

'She and her husband, Picton, have their own self-contained cottage behind the house. He looks after the grounds and she looks after the house. But you're quite safe. From me,' he added.

She flashed him a cutting little look then rubbed her brow wearily. 'I am really tired.'

'Well, why don't we sort out a few things and then you can go to bed?' he suggested gravely.

'Such as? The only thing that needs to be sorted out...' she paused and looked at him standing across the room from her, coffee-cup in hand, his expression inscrutable, which sent a curious little tingle of fear down her spine '...is how to get my car going again so that I can go.'

'I think you should stay, Martha.'

Her eyes widened and her voice caught in her throat. 'N-no——'

'Just listen to me for a moment,' he overrode her with an impatient edge. 'Spend the week with me. At least

let us try to get to know each other better. I can assure
you I won't attempt to make love to you against your
will.'

'Are... are you serious?' she stammered.

'Yes,' he replied shortly.

'But I'm due back at work the day after tomorrow...'
She stopped and bit her lip.

'You don't think, in light of these events, that Yvette
will mind do you?' he queried sardonically.

'But what would we do?' she whispered, and
swallowed.

He smiled an oddly grim little smile. 'What normal
people do when they're on holiday: relax, read, fish,
walk.'

'Why?' she blurted out in a curiously thickened voice.
'So that you can seduce me into being willing?'

He lifted his shoulders in a wry shrug. 'If you're so
set against it, I don't think it would be possible.'

A flood of colour suddenly washed into her cheeks
and she put her hands up to them, appalled, which he
observed before commenting, 'If you do stay, I don't
think we should make this a contest of wills, Martha.
Believe me, I'm too old even to think about *trapping*
anyone into sleeping with me. On the other hand, despite all your denials, it is there between us, but who's
to say it won't go away when we get to know each other
better?' He grimaced and added softly, but with irony,
'It's up to you. So far as your car goes, Picton's a
mechanic and he's already got it going again. So you
could leave whenever you wanted to.'

'Why——? You said something about a battle of
wills—why does it sound as if you're issuing a chal-
lenge?' she countered as some of the shock left her.

'Why?' He looked her over reflectively then smiled
suddenly and quite genuinely and in a way that made

her catch her breath. And he murmured, 'Perhaps that was rather unfair—you're the kind of person that responds to challenges above all else, I guess. I thought it might be more effective than going down on my knees.' But the laughter was still in his eyes.

Martha kept her mouth shut, told herself not to do it but then did it anyway. 'One week,' she said crisply, 'unless I decide to leave earlier, but if it's still no by the end of it——'

'I'm to banish myself forever?' he suggested. 'You have my word.'

'If your word is anything like your aunt's...' Martha tossed her head then realised what she'd done and ran right out of steam. 'I...I...' She gripped her hands.

'All you have to do is go to bed,' he said after a moment of studying her, but with no amusement in his eyes now, and then he turned away abruptly.

She woke up in the yellow-draped bed to a gloriously sunny morning and Grace tapping on the door.

'Brought you breakfast, Miss Winters!'

'Oh, Grace, you shouldn't have!' Martha sat up, yawned, stretched and swept back her hair.

'Well, now, seeing as you had such a day yesterday and didn't eat your dinner, what more could I do?' Grace beamed as she placed the laden tray across Martha's knees. 'Truth to tell, I love having people to cook for and fuss over! Doesn't happen nearly enough these days, which is such a pity for a lovely house like this.' And she bustled about tidying up the clothes Martha had left carelessly draped over the back of a chair the previous night.

'This is a really huge breakfast,' Martha said helplessly a moment later as she surveyed the orange juice, muesli and yoghurt and lifted a silver dome to find bacon, mushrooms and two eggs beneath.

'Aha, but Mr Simon plans to take you fishing on the loch today, and once he starts catching fish there's no telling when he'll stop. Mind you, I've made up a lunch basket——'

'Fishing,' Martha murmured.

'Don't you know how to fish? I wouldn't worry. I expect he wants to dazzle you with how good he is at it.'

'Oh, well, that'll be fine, then, I guess.'

'You've done this before!'

Martha glinted the faintest smile in Simon Macquarie's direction. They were aboard a half cabin cruiser; the waters of the loch were blue and silver around them as they rocked gently in a light breeze; he was dressed in old shorts and an even older, patched shirt; the sun was picking out the gold strands in his hair and on his arms and legs—and his expression was almost comically rueful.

'Once or twice,' she murmured, and went on baiting her hook before she cast the line expertly and gracefully out into the water.

'Why did you let Grace think you were a novice?'

'She told me you probably wanted to dazzle me with your expertise—I didn't want to disillusion her. I also wasn't sure what kind of fishing you had in mind. This is Scotland after all, the land of fly-fishing, waders and trout. I haven't done any of that.'

'I'm relieved to hear there's something I could teach you,' he said wryly. 'Although by the look of your touch you'd pick it up all too quickly. Where did you learn to fish?'

'We had a lake at home . . . until it dried up. And an old dinghy. My father had me catching fish almost before I could walk—— Oh!' She hit her line, reeled in and landed her fourth fish. He had not caught any so far. And she had to laugh for the sheer joy of catching fish on a marvellous morning—as well as his expression. Then she said, 'Perhaps I'd better stop and let you get among them.'

'In case I develop an inferiority complex?' he suggested politely.

She shrugged, still smiling. 'Men don't like to be outdone in these kind of pursuits, do they?'

He considered the matter then said gravely, 'It's a matter of weighing things up, I guess. I should probably get all out of patience if you were one of those girls who hated dirtying their hands or their clothes, who squealed and leapt back from a live fish on a hook, who were intolerably squeamish—so no, I don't mind how many fish you catch, Martha. You're also a sight for sore eyes this morning,' he added, his lips twisting as he surveyed her gleaming, tangled hair, her lack of make-up, her simple navy blue T-shirt and denim shorts, her long golden legs. He went on before she could say anything, 'Tell me something. Do you enjoy modelling?'

'Not always,' she said slowly. 'It can be terribly bitchy and competitive. It can be awfully hard work and it gets a bit soul-destroying when so much emphasis is on the outer you and no one really cares what's going on inside.'

'You have made a couple of statements, though. As a model, I mean.'

Martha grimaced. 'Because I refuse to pout?'

'And refuse to look like a waif, apparently.'

'That's actually good business sense,' Martha said wryly. 'I'm not built like one.'

'What about the pouting?'

'That just doesn't come naturally to me.' And she waited, fully expecting him to take issue.

But all he said after a few minutes silence was, 'So, is modelling more a means to an end for you?'

'I suppose so.'

'And what will you do when you have all the means you need?'

She glanced across at him but the sun was in her eyes; she shaded them with her hand and said a bit flatly, 'I don't know yet. I was all geared up to go on living the life I'd always lived. I... You've got a fish on your line.'

His eyes glinted and he murmured, 'So I have. How fortuitous. OK, back to our competition—you're only three in front now.'

They finished up all square with six fish each, causing Martha to say, 'I think that's appropriate, don't you?' as she helped him to beach the boat on the loch shore below the house. It was mid-afternoon and, as had happened the day before, clouds were building up and threatening rain. All the same she couldn't believe the day had gone so quickly, or, for that matter, so enjoyably.

'Entirely appropriate,' he agreed, but grinned and added, 'I'd have hated like hell to be outdone.'

'I probably shouldn't say this but so would I.'

'Why shouldn't you say it?'

She shrugged. 'I don't know. Well, perhaps I do—I'm trying not to turn this into a contest of wills.'

'Oh, I don't mind this kind of contest,' he drawled.

Martha put her hands on her hips. 'You just said you'd have hated to be outdone!'

'I could have lived with it. There are always other days and other fish.'

'You're—you won't find it so easy to outfish, me, Simon Macquarie,' she said with a mixture of chagrin and amusement.

He'd been bending over, tilting the outboard motor up, and he straightened so that they were standing facing each other, only a couple of inches apart, and laughed down at her. 'And you're—I know I've said this before—but you're stunning, Martha. I even think I like you better like this.'

Martha caught her breath then forced herself to look down wryly. 'I'm a mess.'

'Half the world would give its eye-teeth to look as you do at the moment. Look at me,' he said quietly.

She raised her eyes reluctantly and was immediately struck by the knowledge that it was a mistake. Because she couldn't tear her gaze away and despite the fact that he was as messy as she was everything that had ever tormented her about Simon Macquarie rose up to taunt her again. And she knew, with despair, that he only had to reach out and touch her for her defences to crumble...

Why am I fighting this fight, going through this charade? she wondered bitterly. He's attracted me, he's *always* attracted me as no other man ever has—perhaps the only way to overcome it *is* to... No, don't even think that. Remember instead how you felt when he left you the last time. 'I... what will we do now?' she said with a catch in her voice but her eyes very blue and steady.

She thought he was about to raise a hand just as she'd feared—she saw one fist clench—but he relaxed it almost immediately. And he said, 'Do? What would you like to do? It's about to pour again.'

Her lips curved into a faint smile. 'Curl up with a good book? You did mention reading.'

He grimaced. 'So I did. Why not? I've got a few calls to make.'

So she did just that as the rain thrummed heavily on the roof, in the depths of an armchair with a small fire burning cheerfully in the grate of a sitting-room-cum-study that had been his mother's favourite room, according to Grace.

'It's lovely,' Martha had said when Grace had suggested she use it, looking around at the crammed bookshelves, the pale green armchair covers patterned with full, blowsy pink and white roses, the pink carpet, the antique clocks and porcelain collection.

'She was a lovely lady,' Grace had replied sadly. 'Now you just relax here and I'll bring you afternoon tea.'

'Grace, please, nothing to eat,' Martha had begged. 'I'll be out of a job if you go on feeding me like this.' The picnic basket they'd shared on the boat had been stuffed full of goodies.

'Tosh! You didn't eat much last night.'

So she'd had fragrant Earl Grey tea and one hot scone dripping with butter and honey. Then she'd browsed among the books, found Paul Gallico's *Snow Goose*, which she'd read as a child, and sat down to read it again with a sense of delight.

That was how Simon found her, just closing it, with tears on her lashes.

'Martha?' He stood in front of her looking down interrogatively and holding two glasses.

'It's nothing.' She sniffed. 'Just a lovely book that's like an old friend. What's the time?'

'Nearly dinnertime.'

She groaned. 'Madame won't be at all happy with you if I go back twice my size.'

'We could always walk it off tomorrow,' he suggested. 'If it stops raining. Like a sherry?'

'Thanks.' She took the proffered glass and he sat down opposite her. 'What have you been doing all this time?'

'This and that. Mostly business. I never seem to be able to escape it entirely. I'm off to Japan shortly.'

'Are they...?'

'Outside America, they're our biggest market. They love it.'

'I've always wanted to go to Japan,' Martha said, and bit her lip.

'Why don't you come with me?'

A log crumbled in the grate, the only sound to break the sudden silence until Martha said evenly, 'I think I'll just ignore that.'

He looked amused. 'OK.'

She stood up abruptly and crossed to the window. 'Have you spoken to Madame?'

'Yes.'

'What was her reaction?'

'Complete protestations of innocence, even to the extent of saying that she'd totally forgotten I would be here.'

'She told me you'd *told* her—— Oh, what's the difference?' And she shrugged tautly.

'Martha,' he said from right behind her, 'I believe *you*, not her. What are you all bitter and twisted about now?'

'Nothing!' She swung round, her eyes sparking.

'Then come and have dinner like a good girl,' he said reasonably, causing her to grind her teeth, but, after a brief hesitation, she followed him into the dining-room.

'So she doesn't mind me staying up here for the week?' Martha said during the soup.

'She totally approves.'

'I might have known.'

'Yes, well, we've reasoned all that out, haven't we?'

She cast him a speaking look and made no further conversation until halfway through the grilled fish they'd caught. Not that her silence appeared to affect Simon at all. He ate with the appearance of being completely at ease and comfortable with his own thoughts.

I hate him, Martha thought suddenly. And I can't stand any more of this...

But as if he guessed her thoughts he said abruptly, and with a straight, probing, greeny grey gaze, 'Why don't you *tell* me instead of bottling it all up? Because if you imagine all the trauma is on your side you're wrong.'

'I've never for one moment doubted that,' Martha said cuttingly. 'It's just a pity our traumas don't coincide.'

'We won't know that until we expose them,' he replied meditatively, and reached for his wine.

'All right, you go first!'

'My trauma?' He paused and for a moment his gaze was unseeing as if focused on something far away. Then he said flatly, 'I'm tempted to ask you to marry me, Martha, and thereby short-circuit this whole lengthy process.'

Martha choked and knocked over her wine glass. And Grace must have been hovering because she was through the door like a flash, mopping up, patting Martha on the back and shooting indignant glances at her employer.

Which caused him to grimace wryly and say gravely, 'Thank you, Grace. Would you mind if we missed dessert and went straight to the coffee? Martha is worried about her figure.

'Well?' he drawled, when the transition had been made back to his mother's sitting-room where the fire had been stoked and built up again and the coffee served.

'I think I'm speechless,' Martha murmured dazedly, and discovered that everything she'd done from the time she'd knocked over her wine glass had been achieved like an underwater swimmer or as if in a dream sequence. 'You can't surely be serious?' She raised her eyes to him and they were deep and blue and still stunned.

'Why not?' he shrugged. 'There would appear to be no other way—any that you will allow, at least—to break this paralysing impasse... Because you're terrified I'm going to walk out on you again?' he said softly but with the kind of precision that was like a dart shooting straight home.

'I...I'm...I have no idea whether we *love* each other!' Martha protested, gathering some resources at last.

'Well, what's your idea of love, then?' he queried placidly. 'Do tell me.'

She paled and whispered, 'I don't think it's the same as yours somehow, Simon.'

'Yet you've allowed no man to touch you since I left you. So what *is* it, then—for you?' And his gaze was suddenly merciless, his mouth set grimly.

She flushed brilliantly. 'Don't do this to...' She stopped and put a hand to her mouth.

'Don't do this to you?' he mocked. 'I'm banging my head up against a brick wall any other way.'

'Well—but it's not your business——'

'Of course it is,' he said roughly. 'And I've now made my intentions clear.'

'But that's as good as saying, If I can't have you any other way, I'll marry you!' Martha cried.

'Exactly.' There was a tinge of derision in his eyes now. 'I don't know why but I quite got the impression that that was what was required of me.'

'Oh! I——'

'My dear Martha, you say there is no pride involved,' he continued relentlessly, 'you refuse most of my overtures, although you still melt in my arms and kiss me like a woman who is starved——' He stopped as she leapt up as if to attack him but he didn't even flinch, just raised an ironic eyebrow at her.

Sense prevailed but it came with a burning sense of shame—until he said drily, 'I'm sorry there are no daisies for you to shred.'

She breathed deeply and tossed her head with anger now coursing through her veins. But with something else as well, she discovered only moments later—a sense of inner unease because he was right about so much and to go on fighting him like this when he knew her so well just didn't sit squarely with her any more. In fact it was worse; it was humiliating and as if she was letting herself down...

Her shoulders slumped briefly, then she squared them resolutely with a new kind of pride and lifted her face, pale again and with the sheen of tears glittering against the dark blue of her eyes, and said, 'I won't marry you—I wouldn't marry anyone in these circumstances but I can't go on fighting you like this. It's not honest.'

She held her breath, waiting to be demolished as his expression didn't change, seemed carved in stone in fact, but then he put out a hand, took one of hers and said barely audibly at last, 'Thank you for that.' And he drew her into his arms.

Martha trembled as their bodies touched and said foolishly, 'Will it be now—tonight, I mean?'

He kissed her throat and her hair and his hands roamed her back and her hips. 'Only if you want it to be. Not if you're thinking, I might as well get this over and done with.'

She had to smile against his shoulder. 'I wasn't but——'

'I know.' His arms tightened around her. 'It's a big step. Would you like to be courted for a day or so more?'

Martha hesitated then said with resolution, 'No. That sounds coy and girlish and...not very fair so——'

But he stilled her words with his mouth on hers and when she next spoke she was lying in his arms on the settee, reduced to a nearly mindless state of rapture. 'I've thought about this for so long,' she whispered, and winced.

'Go on.'

'No, it's embarrassing.' She turned her face away.

'Martha,' he said gently, tilting her chin so that he could look into her eyes, 'let's let there be no more embarrassment between us. But I don't want to rush you.'

'Right now I feel as if I'm on a runaway train,' she said, and shivered as his fingers strayed beneath her blouse.

He smiled and kissed her lightly. 'That makes two of us. You're——' his voice became curiously unsteady as he unbuttoned her blouse and the firelight flickered over her skin '—more beautiful than ever.'

'Simon...?'

'Mmm?' He raised his head from her breasts. They were lying together on the yellow bed, unclothed, and he'd touched and stroked her for a long time with care and consideration until she'd started to relax and give herself over to the delight he was inflicting on her. And she'd thought dimly once that something else was taking place together with the slow drift of his hands and lips on her skin and the unlocking of sources of sheer, intimate joy with a touch so light, yet sure. It was as if he was persuading her to surrender her well-being into his hands, to let down the last barriers... She also thought as his lean, strong body touched hers, Will I ever be the same again? Not only because I'll never be a virgin again but I'll be his and my well-being will always depend on him...

'Martha?' He propped his head on his hand and looked down at her but his other hand never left her body and his fingers sought the satiny hollows at the base of her throat then slid down in the upcurve of her breast, and further along the swell of her hip, and all the time he scanned the paler curves of her figure, the triangle of curls below the slight mound of her stomach, the long sweep of her legs. Until finally his eyes came back to hers and his fingers plucked one nipple then the other.

A shudder went through Martha and in a convulsive movement she buried her face in his chest and whispered, 'It's too much ... Please.'

But he tilted her chin again and kissed her deeply before he eased his weight on to her and finally possessed her.

CHAPTER SIX

'MARTHA?'

'Yes?' she said drowsily, and moved her cheek on Simon Macquarie's arm before starting up abruptly, realising she was naked and lying back hurriedly, clutching the sheet to her.

He laughed softly and cradled her body to his. 'Forget where you were?' he murmured against the side of her mouth.

'Yes,' she admitted ruefully. 'I mean...' She stopped and, as he said no more, bit by bit discovered all over again the unfamiliar yet wonderful feeling she'd woken up to: the warmth, the contentment, the sense of sharing and contact. And she moved her body luxuriously against his and smiled dreamily. 'What I mean is I feel like a cat who's got the cream.'

'I'm very glad to hear that,' he replied gravely.

'Oh?'

'Yes. It's entirely appropriate for one thing and a great boast to my ego for another. But no, seriously,' he added as she started to laugh, and he smoothed her hair off her face and looked into her blue eyes with no humour in his now, 'I hope it didn't hurt too much.'

Martha caught her breath as she remembered the one tense, tearing moment and how he'd held her and said her name and carried her over it with infinite gentleness. 'No,' she said softly. 'No more than it should have, thanks to you. I don't think what followed could have happened otherwise, do you?'

He stared down at her still with that intent look then kissed her and lay back. 'I'm glad there are no morning-after-the-night-before regrets.'

Martha propped herself on one elbow. 'Did you think there would be?'

His lips twisted. 'It's been a long, rocky road. Yes, I did wonder.'

'Perhaps I made a long, rocky road for myself,' she said slowly, and grimaced. 'In the light of this day, I wouldn't blame you for thinking that.'

'Martha——' he turned on his side and faced her squarely '—whatever happens from here, I did you a grave injustice three years ago and I compounded it when we met again, whereas you...' He stopped and for a moment his eyes were unusually bleak. 'Whereas I have to salute you, Martha Winters,' he said.

There was a curious, heart-stoppingly tense little pause as they stared into each other's eyes. Why? Martha wondered. What is he really saying?

But then the moment was gone as he pulled her down and buried his face between her breasts.

It took her two days to find the answer to that question.

'This walking,' she said in the afternoon. 'I'm not *that* worried about my figure.' They were trudging hand in hand up a rocky path beside the loch; there was the fragrant smell of lemon thyme and damp earth on the air and the sun was shining from a clear blue sky and dancing on the ruffled waters below.

He stopped and swung her to face him.

'What?' she murmured, not entirely sure about the gravity of his expression.

'I just thought I should warn you that any reference to your figure could have unexpected consequences.'

She started to smile. 'Not here—out in the open for anyone to see, surely?'

'Look around, Martha,' he replied softly. 'There's not a soul for miles.'

'Well——' she did look around and she swallowed suddenly at the preoccupied, heavy-lidded way he was studying her when she looked back '—you're not serious?' she said uncertainly.

'Entirely serious.'

'But . . .'

'About kissing you here and now,' he murmured.

'Oh, that——' She stopped.

'That's OK? Thank you, ma'am,' he responded. 'I'll try not to overstep the bounds of propriety, ma'am.' And he took her in his arms.

When he released her about five minutes later, she was breathless and her cheeks were pink and he laughed down into her eyes. 'I think that will have to do for the moment, don't you?' he said softly.

But before she got the chance to reply a party of three hikers rounded the bend below them, causing her to feel even hotter. And when they'd passed with cheery greetings she said, 'Not a soul for miles, you said?'

'I miscalculated,' he replied wryly. 'Anyway, I think we should go home now. This place is not only over-populated but lacking in certain comforts for what I really have in mind.'

Martha blushed again, which he observed with a smile lurking in his eyes. 'But only with your permission, naturally,' he added.

She discovered two things: that to have him standing so close and looking at her the way he was made her feel weak at the knees and be invaded by memories of the hard strength and suppleness of his body, and what he had done to hers; and, secondly, that if she wasn't careful she would give the impression of being a tongue-tied, hot-headed, foolish, star-struck young girl. So she said, although huskily, 'Permission granted, Mr Macquarie. I agree with your observations.'

But he didn't move immediately. Instead he lifted his hands to run them through her hair and then straighten the collar of her blouse before he touched her mouth lightly. Then he said quietly, 'If what I do to you is anything like what you do to me, Martha, we're in this together.'

'I...' she winced at his perspicacity '...I just didn't want to seem gauche, I guess.'

'Your idea of gaucheness is not the same as mine. The way you are delights me, in fact.'

'Well—thanks,' she whispered and then her lips curved into a smile. 'I'll try not to run all the way home, however.'

He laughed and, talking of delight, she thought that Simon Macquarie, like this, delighted *her* as they turned and began to climb down the hill.

But Grace was waiting to meet them when they got back to the house, all in a flutter. 'Something's up,' she said dramatically. 'The phone doesna' stop ringing, that fax thing is going beserk and I can't understand half of the calls because they're speaking French!'

Simon glanced ruefully at Martha before saying something soothing to Grace. Then he turned back to her, raised her hand which he was holding to his lips and said, 'Why don't you have a rest before dinner? Whatever this is may take a little sorting out if we're to get any peace.'

Grace said immediately, 'An excellent idea! Come along, Miss Winters. I'll bring you up a pot of tea!'

And it was Grace Martha was thinking of once she'd finished her tea and been left in peace to rest in the yellow bedroom. Grace, who had accepted the turn of events which Simon had made no attempt to hide with perfect composure. So that the awkwardness Martha had felt hadn't been necessary at all. I wonder why? she mused as she lay on the bed in her underclothes beneath a light cover and also reflected that for someone who never took a rest during the day this wasn't a bad idea ...

But her thoughts returned to Grace and then, as if by natural progression, to Madame. Why are both of them pushing me like this? Well, not Grace so much but Madame certainly and even Grace is happy. It's almost as if they desperately want to find a wife for Simon—or am I imagining it? And she suddenly felt a bit hot and cold at the same time. But no, take it logically, she persisted. I'm perfectly sure that Grace is a respectable old lady through to her bones, and, even fond as she obviously is of Simon, she would not condone this lightly. She might put up with it because she has no choice, she might be polite and correct, but she wouldn't, I'm sure, make me feel so cherished, unless... As for Madame, she is without doubt pushing me, with every conniving trick she can come up with, into his arms. Why...?

But as no answer came she pulled a pillow into her arms and fell asleep.

It was nearly dinnertime when she woke and the house was quiet and peaceful. She got up and had a shower and had just stepped out with a towel in her hand when the partly opened bathroom door widened and Simon stood there.

She experienced a moment of confusion, dropping the towel then tripping as she bent to retrieve it and finding him there before her and removing it from her fingers. She straightened and took an uncertain breath, her skin still rosy, sleek and wet, her hair dripping, her nipples suddenly flowering beneath his intent gaze.

'Martha,' he said barely audibly, 'how the hell am I going to resist this?' And he too dropped the towel and put his hands on her waist then curved them upwards to cup her breasts. 'You're beautiful,' he said.

She gazed up into his eyes and her colour fluctuated deliciously at the naked desire she saw in them. 'Thank you,' she murmured.

He said something beneath his breath and took his hands away. Then, 'I have to go to Edinburgh tonight. Come, I'll tell you about it while you get dressed. I would——' his lips quirked '—offer to dry you but that would place an intolerable strain on my will-power.' And he handed her the towel.

So, somewhat dazedly, she dried herself hurriedly and wrapped the towel round her. She followed Simon into the bedroom and discovered he'd brought two sherries with him. He handed her one and said without preamble, 'There's been a crisis—some strange movements in our shares on the stock-market that could herald a take-over bid or could be pure coincidence. Whatever, I've had to convene a directors' meeting in Edinburgh this evening in about two hours' time. Don't stand there in that damp towel,' he added.

'I...' Martha sipped her sherry more for something to do than anything else. 'I'm all right.'

'I'd like to watch you getting dressed,' he said softly.

'That might not be—what I mean is...' She broke off and bit her lip.

'Might not do my will-power any good? It mightn't,' he agreed. 'I'd like to be able to grin and bear it, however.' A wicked little smile glinted her way.

'Well...' She paused uncertainly.

'Humour me, Martha,' he said softly.

So she put her glass down carefully and dropped the towel. Nor did he say another word as she put her bra and panties on then a short-sleeved jumper the colour of cornflowers and a pair of indigo jeans. Finally, breathing erratically beneath his never-wavering gaze, she sat down at the dressing-table and clasped her hands together awkwardly.

And she said as he moved at last and brought her her sherry, and stayed standing behind her as their gazes caught and held in the mirror with an odd little query in his eyes, 'I hope you don't think I'm being pretentious.'

'Why should I think that?'

'Well, I've paraded in enough swimsuits, but I've never done that before.'

For a moment something fleetingly grim and bleak touched his expression, then he said, 'I'm sorry if I made you feel exposed. The thing is, I'm cursing like hell inwardly at having to leave you so soon like this. And I'm probably rushing my fences because of it. It's all so new for you, isn't it?' He lifted up a strand of her hair, stared down at it then looked into her eyes in the mirror. 'I tend to forget.'

She closed her eyes and breathed in relief that he'd understood. She laid her head gratefully back against his waist. 'When are you going?'

'In about ten minutes. There's a helicopter coming to pick me up. I'll be home tomorrow but I'm not sure what time. Grace will look after you.'

'I'm sure she will,' Martha murmured, and he bent and kissed her lips gently.

'Grace, tell me a bit about Simon,' Martha said the next afternoon.

They were sitting in the back garden; Martha was shelling peas—she'd insisted on being allowed to help with dinner—and Grace was polishing away at an old copper jug. A tea-tray with a plate of home-made biscuits was on the table between them, and the back garden, which was the herb garden, was warm and sunny and alive with birdsong and redolent with a minty fragrance.

'Mr Simon?' Grace said slowly, and looked into the distance for a moment. 'I've known him since he was a boy; a lovely lad he was too. Such a pity.'

Martha waited patiently as she shelled peas.

'His Mum and Da' didn't get on, you see, which isn't easy to grow up with, and I can't help wondering if it didn't make him a bit hard and cynical sometimes. Then, when he did fall in love with a wonderful girl—three or four years ago it would have been—one week before the wedding she was killed in a car accident. I don't think he's been serious about another woman since,' Grace said. Then she flushed, recovered and added, 'Saving yourself, perhaps.'

Martha, who'd been staring at Grace with her mouth open, suddenly poured herself another cup of tea. 'Did you...did you ever meet Sondra Grant, Grace?' she asked diffidently, hating herself a little for what she was doing but compelled all the same.

'I did. I liked her,' Grace said forthrightly, 'but he wasna' in love with her.'

'How could you tell?'

Grace smiled. 'I saw him with Morag, don't forget. I saw the two of them together often enough, right here.'

'And...me?'

Grace lifted her wrinkled face beneath its snowy white hair and stared right into Martha's eyes. 'He could be, lassie,' she said gently. 'I don't know yet—do you?'

'No,' Martha whispered. 'So, would it be fair to say, Grace, that you'd love to see him married?'

'That I would,' Grace agreed. 'Picton and I have no children so we look upon him as the son we never had. And it's no good even if he thinks he can't forget her for him not to try to make a life with someone else. He'll never forget her that way.'

'I think he might have been going to try with Sondra.'

'Maybe,' Grace conceded. 'She certainly had hopes but I don't know if she understood him at all.'

Martha flinched. She said, 'I hope you don't mind me asking these things but...well, you sort of welcomed me with open arms and I couldn't help wondering why.'

Grace shrugged and started to polish vigorously again. 'I like who I like and it often only takes me two minutes to decide. Anyway, you're the dead opposite of her and that's why I thought—well...' Grace said awkwardly, and was apparently unable to go on so she resumed polishing fiercely.

Martha nearly choked on a sip of tea. 'Who?'

Grace sighed, 'Morag, lassie. Who he was engaged to.'

'Could you—would you please tell me how, Grace? No one else has even mentioned her to me, you see, and I...' She stopped.

Grace stopped polishing too and observed how Martha was clenching her hands, and she shrugged suddenly. 'I don't think that's fair. She was a redhead with fantastic yellow eyes. But she wasn't beautiful the way you are: a bit shorter, thinner yet she had the kind of vitality that was breathtaking and she was marvellously eloquent. She talked to everyone; she could talk about anything; she was very brainy and there wasn't a shy bone in her body. She was sort of witty and wise. You could never be bored with her. Everyone sought her for their parties, men flocked after her—well, until she and Simon got engaged. She was—she just put everyone under her spell. She was like the belle of the ball down in London, apparently, and it was going to be *the* wedding of the season,' Grace said a little helplessly. She went on, 'The only reason I'm telling this is because you looked so confused and I've got the feeling you really love Simon and it might help you a bit to understand him.'

Simon didn't come home that day. He rang to say tomorrow for sure but he couldn't say what time. And Martha lay in bed that night still reeling from Grace's confidences and wondering what difference they made. Of course, it now made sense why people had looked at her as they had and possibly explained why the gossip columns had been so titillated... Had everyone been thinking the same—that she couldn't be more different from Morag, not only in looks but in her reserve? Had that been what had motivated Madame—a girl who couldn't possibly remind him of his dead love? His losing someone he loved a week before his wedding had to account for the darkness she herself had sometimes seen in him, even in Sydney when it must have still been very close to him. Would it be enough for him that she didn't remind him of his lost love? Would it be enough for her? Was that what he'd meant when he'd said something only days ago, something that had stuck in her mind about Yvette and the *other* reason she would have for pushing them together? And, 'Whatever happens from here...' he'd said two days ago. A make-do marriage? she wondered.

She was out walking late in the afternoon when he did get home the next day, so she had no warning. Discarding her shoes outside the back door and walking through the house to go up to her bedroom, she ran right into him.

'Oh! Simon!'

'Martha,' he responded, steadying her with his hands on her waist, taking in her pink cheeks, her wind-blown hair, her jeans and anorak. 'I was wondering where you'd got to,' he murmured. 'It's not exactly walking weather unless you like battling the elements.'

'I do sometimes,' she confessed, but did not add that the state of her mind somewhat resembled the blustery elements and she'd been doing battle with that as much as anything.

But his eyes narrowed as if he detected some tension and he released her, but took her hand and said briefly, 'Come in here.'

He led her into his mother's sitting-room, closed the door, turned to her again and said, 'I know exactly what you need—I've been away too long.'

'No—I mean you couldn't help it,' Martha said as he took her in his arms.

'And I haven't been away too long?' A wicked glint lit his eyes as he gazed down at her. 'It's been too long for me, I can assure you. It's been not only the sex, although that's been a torment, but too little togetherness so far.' He paused then said very quietly, 'It's been a lost, lonely sort of feeling.'

Martha's eyes widened and something like an overtaut spring inside her started to wind down as she whispered, 'That's exactly... How did you know?'

He cupped her face and kissed her gently. 'I'm not a monster, really. Come.' And he picked her up and sat down with her in an armchair. 'New lovers get that way and you'd have to agree we're very, very new.'

She laid her head against his shoulder and rubbed her cheek on the wool of his Arran sweater. 'What about old lovers?' she said, and bit her lip.

He was silent for a long time but he stroked her hair rhythmically until he said, 'Do you want to talk about that now, Martha?'

'No. I . . . no. I think it is all too new,' she said. 'Could you kiss me, please?'

'Why not?' he said slowly, and did just that.

'You do realise,' he said some time later, and took away his hand, which had been lying on her breast beneath her jumper, to glance at his watch, 'that we're about to be doomed again.'

She smiled softly. 'Dinner?'

'Uh-huh. We've played havoc with a few of Grace's dinners.'

'There is the whole night, though,' she pointed out. 'After dinner.'

'There is. I'll just have to be strong.' And the silver bell tinkled right on cue.

'And I haven't changed or anything!' She sat up and ran her hands through her hair.

But he said wryly. 'You never need to.'

'I would like to wash my hands and brush my hair, though.'

'OK—I'll meet you in the dining-room.'

Grace served up *coq au vin* after mushroom soup and a chocolate mousse for dessert. For once they did justice to her meal although Martha only had a tiny portion of dessert—just enough for Grace to pronounce herself pleased.

And they were still chuckling, as they drank their coffee in the sitting-room, to think that they'd finally finished a meal together.

Then Martha said, 'I haven't asked you about—whatever the problem was. Not that I'm prying or anything,' she added quickly. 'I just hope it went well.'

He lay back in his chair, stretched his long legs towards the fire and said lazily, 'It went well. I won't bore you with the details—it took a little fancy footwork——' he looked amused '— but it's good to be kept on your toes.'

Martha watched him through her lashes for a moment and discovered her heart beating oddly because there seemed to be so much latent power in him at that moment—a man to whom a possible take-over of his company was all in a day's work. What chance did I have of ever fighting him and winning? she thought with a sudden sharp little breath, and said, to cover it, 'Tell me a bit about cognac.'

'Well,' he mused, 'it's a funny thing about cognac, made in Cognac, France from French grapes et cetera, but most of the major companies were started by foreigners. Otard was another Scot, Hennessey was an Irishman.'

'That must irritate the French a bit.'

He grimaced. 'I think it might irritate me if I were fully French. But, to cut a long story short, it starts out as wine fermented from white grapes grown in six areas around Cognac—and those areas are defined by law. It's called *eau-de-vie*; then when it gets to the distillery it's heated to boiling-point and the vapour that rises passes through what they call a swan's neck, a narrow curved pipe, and then a spiral coil that passes through cold water so that the vapour condenses again. The following day it goes through the same procedure and comes out as one hundred and forty proof Cognac *eau-de-vie*.'

'Wow!'

'Mmm.' He grinned. 'Pretty potent stuff.'

'So how does it get to the drinkable stage?'

'It's stored in specially made oak casks, the longer the better, and the tannin from the oak gets absorbed, giving it its amber colour, and it slowly loses its fire and gains bouquet and aroma. The older the casks are, the better the cognac. But perhaps the most important ingredient for fine cognac is a discerning cellar-master. It's his job to blend the different *eau-de-vie* and it's generally a job that is handed down from father to son.'

'Like perfume—I mean, you need to be born with the nose—or in this case the palate, I guess.'

'You guess right although both palate and nose are involved in cognac.'

'So how long does your family's involvement with this go back?'

'To the late 1700s.'

Martha grimaced. 'I don't know much about my family beyond my grandparents.'

'Are your parents still alive?'

'No,' she said slowly. 'It was such a blow for them to lose the farm that although I was able to help them a bit once I started to model they never really recovered. They died within three months of each other.'

'And you have no brothers or sisters?'

'No.' She smiled. 'I was a belated only child too, after years and years of trying. That's also why I'm such a whiz at huntin', fishin', ridin' and so on. My father always treated me like a son.'

He looked at her curiously. 'Didn't you mind?'

'Oh, no! He was rather sweet about it... Did you think I might be harbouring dark, deep traumas because of it?'

'No,' he said slowly. 'But you are independent and fiery sometimes.'

'I think I was born that way,' Martha said with a toss of her head and a wry little smile. 'But you also just happened to catch me at a bad time.'

'Talking of times,' he said after a moment, 'would this be a bad time to suggest we go to bed? We've observed the proprieties—it's even almost dark.'

Her lips quirked. 'Why not?'

'Simon?'

'Yes—are you laughing by the way?' he queried.

Martha looked down and ran her fingers through his hair. 'I was,' she said softly. 'I was just thinking that there's nothing very fiery or independent about me now.'

He raised his head. She was sitting on her heels on the bed in the circle of his arms and he'd taken off all her clothes bar her bra, as well as all of his. The last light of day was fading fast and he reached out and switched on the bedside lamp. 'On the other hand,' he said barely audibly, 'why should you be when you can bowl me over this way? I've been tormenting myself for two days, thinking about doing this.' And he reached round her and released her bra.

She caught her breath as he slid it down her arms and freed her breasts. Then he took his hands from her body but feasted his eyes on her until she moved and slid her hands down her thighs in a self-conscious little gesture.

'Still shy?' he said with that heavy-lidded look she was coming to know. 'You shouldn't be—you're exquisite. Your breasts are like beautiful firm fruit tinted gold and honey, and your hips are a work of art. As for your legs—do you know how that long-legged stalk of yours affects me sometimes?'

She licked her lips and said huskily, 'I think I'd prefer you to hold me when you say those kind of things——'

'God, Martha——' his voice was suddenly as husky as hers as he interrupted her and swept her into his arms abruptly '—how the hell I've held off holding you, held off through dinner and all the rest, is something of a mystery.' And he buried his face in her hair. 'How the hell I held off three years ago is also a mystery.'

And it was she who said, 'Hush,' as she felt the spasm of his muscles and the tautness of his body. 'Let's not go back.'

'You're right—there's only one way for me *to* go, unfortunately,' he said wryly, and lay back with her at last. 'Do you mind?'

'Of course not,' she whispered, and thought that she loved this blend of impatience with his patience and understanding of earlier. But then when he claimed her with a mixture of power and control that brought her to an indescribably lovely, star-shot climax she amended that in her mind, as she clung to him for strength and support, to simply loving him ...

But the next morning he was not beside her in bed when she woke. He was up and dressed and standing across the room, his shoulders propped against the wall, watching her.

She sat up slowly, ran a hand through her hair and reached for her nightgown, feeling at the same time a cold finger of fear run down her spine as he said nothing, just continued to watch her, his expression indecipherable.

'Simon?' She slipped the nightgown over her head. 'Is something wrong? Do you have to go away again?' She freed her hair from the neck of the nightgown.

'No—Martha, do you regret sleeping with me at all?'

Her eyes widened and she put her hands together uncertainly. 'No—how could I? Why are you asking, though? Have I done something wrong?'

'On the contrary—there are some things you do almost too well. So I think it's foolish for us to beat about the bush. Will you marry me?'

CHAPTER SEVEN

'No...'

He moved at last. 'No? Just like that?'

'Simon——' Martha discovered she was clenching her fists and her voice was hoarse with uncertainty '—why are you doing this? I mean...' She stopped as he strolled over to the bed and stood looking down at her, his hands shoved into his pockets. And she shivered because his eyes were dark and unreadable; in fact his whole aura was so different.

'It's not going to be any better with anyone else, you know,' he said coolly. 'It doesn't come much better than that and I've had a bit of experience of it, believe me.'

Martha thought, This is like a nightmare. 'Stop it,' she whispered. 'You're denigrating it when you talk like that—*why*?'

'You don't think you're denigrating it by sleeping with me the way you do but not agreeing to marry me? After being in love with me for three years,' he said with a lethal sort of gentleness that cut her to the quick.

What to say? she wondered desperately. How could he have changed overnight—and why? She said, 'Something's happened—please tell me. This just doesn't make sense.'

'It makes excellent sense to me. Why delay the inevitable——?'

'Who's to say it's inevitable?' she cried, goaded past good sense. 'Who's to say that once this kind of passion cools we don't find ourselves hating each other? Or that you find I *can't* replace your dead love, even though I'm so different!' And she stared up at him defiantly but with tears in her eyes.

'So I was right,' he murmured. 'I thought you were uptight about something else yesterday afternoon. Now I know why.'

'What do you mean?'

'I got up this morning to put an early call through to Edinburgh, whereupon Grace decided to tell me she might have been indiscreet the day before—apparently it had been worrying her all night. But I'm asking you to marry me because of you, not anything to do with Morag,' he said drily, and added abruptly, 'Nor am I prepared to spend another three years talking about it while you make up your mind. Listen——' he sat down at last and prised her hands apart then took her in his arms '—we'll suit each other, I promise you. We always did in this respect—let me show you.'

His kiss was deep; he gave her no chance to evade it and her lips were crushed but she was breathless, her heart was beating heavily, and there was something so sensual between them when he stopped kissing her at last it was almost tangible. Or like an electric current, she thought dazedly, that linked their minds even when their bodies weren't touching, that made her nerves leap and quiver and her body ache with desire.

'I...' she whispered. 'Oh, God, I don't know what to say!'

'Say yes,' he said, and smiled faintly for the first time at the same time as he pushed the shoulder-strap of her nightgown down and touched her exposed breast and the crushed velvet of her nipple delicately. 'I promise you I'll do everything in my power to make sure you don't regret it.'

'And if I still say no?' Martha whispered.

He took his hand away. 'Then there's no point in going on like this, but why would you say no?'

'So we could get to know each other better—— I . . .' She stopped and stared at him a little wildly.

His lips twisted. 'What more do you want to know about me? We enjoy each other's company—do you think you could have spent six hours fishing with a man whose company you *didn't* enjoy?'

She saw the amusement in his eyes and bit her lip.

'I think that's quite a test,' he continued wryly. 'I don't think I have any exceptionally bad habits but if you've noticed any you need only to point them out and I'll try to rectify them.'

'Simon,' she pleaded.

He smiled faintly down at her. 'This is serious? You're right. Are you wondering what kind of a life we would lead? I wouldn't mind if you wanted to keep on modelling for a while. I wouldn't expect you to leave Yvette in the lurch—so long as it didn't take you away from me and so long as you could come away with me when I travel. I'd be delighted when you wanted to start a family and if you could be happy living here I would arrange my life so that we spent most of it here—this estate is crying out for some care and attention, incidentally. You may have noticed that parts of it are bracken-infested and I have sheep roaming all over the hills, a lot of which I didn't even know existed . . . But perhaps the best way I could put it is to point out the alternative. Do you really want to continue what must have been a lonely life, doing something you don't altogether believe in, when we could share all this? Do you really want to have the whole world at your feet below a catwalk or staring at you on the cover of *Vogue*, and only caring about how you look?'

It was a telling, even cruel point and she took a shaken breath as it thrust home. Then she thought, But no, what I really care about, Simon, is this. Do you love me? Are you really filled with it as I am, unfortunately? Or are you trying to replace Morag in your life, or, perhaps even worse, making do with second-best? Will I ever be able to take away that darkness that overcomes you sometimes? Can I make you say the words—what's the point if I don't know whether to believe you?

She looked down abruptly then closed her eyes at the image of her naked breast and his lean, strong hand lying on the sheet at her waist, and realised in a split-second that if she'd found it hard to bear another man's arms around her without actually sleeping with Simon Macquarie it would be impossible to bear now. So if you can't have everything, perhaps you make the best of things, she thought. Perhaps you never give up hope but you understand. And perhaps you remember that this man has been on your mind and in your heart for so long...

'Yes...'

They were to be married in five days' time and other than Grace and Picton not a soul Martha knew knew about it.

Indeed, she got the feeling that if he could have arranged it sooner he would have, and that perhaps it was only some fleeting bewilderment she might have shown in her eyes that had made him organise it in a beautiful little stone church on the island which Grace was to fill with flowers rather than a register office, and made him take her to Edinburgh to buy a special dress.

He did say with a lurking smile in his eyes as they drove back to Mull, with the dress he hadn't seen carefully packed in a box in the boot, 'Yvette will probably kill me.'

'Because she doesn't know and isn't coming?' Martha said after a slight hesitation.

He shrugged. 'That too but I was thinking more of you getting married in a dress other than of her devising.' He paused then took his hand off the wheel, laid it over hers and said quite naturally, 'I don't know if Grace told you *all* the details but Morag's mother had planned this big wedding in London with all the trimmings. It was an exhausting process without, of course, having to call it off the way we had to.'

And Martha's hand curled round his in sudden gratitude. 'I understand,' she said softly. 'And I haven't really got any one close so... apart from Madame.'

'She'll forgive you. It was she who sent you to me after all. Anyway, she's in Bahrain.'

Martha lifted a quizzical eyebrow. 'What on earth is she doing there?'

'Heaven alone knows but it'd like to bet it's something to do with fashion. You could find her next collection including yashmaks.'

'Beautiful,' Grace said with tears in her eyes, standing back.

'Thanks,' Martha said gruffly, and took a last fleeting look at herself in the mirror. The dress was just above ankle-length and fashioned from a pearly silk taffeta embossed with tiny flowers. The neckline was heart-shaped, the sleeves were puffed and elbow-length, the rest a simple A-line design that flowed down her figure and swirled around her legs. And she wore her hair loose with nothing in it. But as she looked away from the mirror and twisted the engagement ring she'd chosen from the selection Simon had presented her with in

Edinburgh—a pear-shaped diamond set on a gold band, the price of which had nearly taken her breath away— her eyes were shadowed and she said simply, 'But, Grace, I don't know if I'm doing the right thing.'

'My dear,' Grace replied, equally simply, 'sometimes you do what you have to do—if you love a man.' Then she stood on her tiptoes and kissed Martha warmly before she added, 'I'm with you, dinna forget.' And the older woman left the room to be driven to the church by Simon.

But on the seat of the Jaguar in which Picton was to drive Martha there was the most beautiful bouquet of tight creamy rosebuds and starry little daisies. 'For you,' Picton said unnecessarily, but added, 'From Mr Simon.' And as if he sensed the emotion of the moment he talked all the way to the church, telling her that he'd brought his camera, with which he was extremely adept because he was an avid bird-watcher and recorder of them, although she might not know it, so she'd be sure to have some great pictures to hand down to posterity. And he went on to tell her about all the birds he'd captured on film.

But she was still filled with nerves and tension as she walked down the short aisle on Picton's arm, until Simon turned. Then she couldn't deny that for a brief moment his greeny grey eyes, as they rested on her, were a little stunned—and it gave her the courage she so desperately needed.

'So this is the surprise honeymoon—France,' she murmured as they boarded a Bordeaux-bound flight later that day.

'Yes.' He linked his fingers through hers. 'I have a cottage in Charente—we'll be entirely on our own. Do you cook?'

She glanced at him. 'Do you?'

'In a limited kind of way.'

'Oh.'

'Martha?'

She looked at the slight tinge of consternation in his expression, and relented. 'Yes, I cook. Very well as it happens—I can even make bread. My mother didn't allow my father to get away with treating me as a son entirely.'

He laughed. 'That's a relief. Mind you, we could have eaten out, I suppose, but it wasn't quite what I had in mind.'

'So I'm to be a prisoner as well as the cook for the next week?' she said with mock-severity.

His lips quirked. 'You can tell me what you think about that, and France, on the way home.'

France? she thought as they flew back to London a week later and she found her nerves tightening at the thought of what lay ahead. Well, Charente—trees and meadows filled with poppies and wild flowers. Fields of cut hay rolled into great round wads, bumble-bees and dragon flies. Sleek, bulky brown cattle, streams and dabchicks. Little medieval villages with narrow, winding streets, old, cold churches and bright canvas awnings above the *charcuterie*, the *boulangerie* and the *boucherie*. Stone barns with roses climbing up their grey walls—roses everywhere—and geraniums and pansies in window-boxes and pots on front steps as well as lavender bushes, hydrangeas, daisies and dahlias. People carrying long, unwrapped bread sticks, wonderful fruit and vegetables—impossible conversations when she got separated from Simon who spoke French like a native. Cognac and the tour of the distillery he'd taken her on, as well as Limoges where she'd confided her fascination with porcelain, pottery and ceramics, and how she'd been quite good at art at school and sometimes wondered about a career involving art and ceramics.

And his two-hundred-year-old partially restored farmhouse set on a rise outside a tiny village amid acres of fields and woods where cuckoos nested and nightingales sang. With its thick grey walls, white-washed interior, fascinating attic and old chestnut floors, its huge fireplace and pair of cherrywood beds, one of which never got used...

Being made love to whenever the mood took him, being absolutely alone with him, cooking for him, sleeping beside him...

'So?'

Martha looked down at his fingers once more entwined with hers, knew he'd read her mind and trembled inwardly. 'It was wonderful—thanks,' she said huskily.

'You don't have to say that.'

'Yes, I do.'

'Are we having our first disagreement as a married couple?' he queried.

She glanced at him but could see only that bland query echoed in his eyes. 'Not that I know of. What do you mean?'

'I mean that you did as much to make it a wonderful honeymoon as I did, therefore no thanks are required.'

'Well—but I couldn't have taken you anywhere as magical as that. So my thanks stand.'

'I see,' he murmured. 'Don't you feel married to me yet, Martha?'

In my heart perhaps *always*, she thought, but otherwise—do I? Or do I sometimes wonder when I'm going to wake up? She tried another tack. 'This is a curious conversation—I'm not sure what you're trying to make me say.'

'I'm not trying to make you say anything; I'm just wondering why you're tense again.'

Her fingers moved involuntarily in his. 'I...don't even know where you live. There's Madame to face. I suppose that's why.'

'But you're not alone in any of those things, Martha.'

'No—does she know?'

'No.'

'Does anyone know?'

'Martha, look at me,' he said intently. When she did at last, he went on, 'Is it anyone's business but our own?'

'No. I'm sorry,' she said very quietly. 'Perhaps all this is just going to take a bit more getting used to.'

'May I make a suggestion, then?'

'What?'

'When you have doubts like this, think of us in bed together.'

Shock made her look fleetingly into his eyes, but long enough to detect the mixture of desire and a certain devilish little glint, before she turned her head to look out of the window as a tide of colour poured into her cheeks and her hand trembled in his.

'I love it when I make you blush,' he said idly. 'I would love it even more if we were in bed together right now; I would love to be making you arch your beautiful body and saying my name the way you sometimes do, as if I was the last spar in the world you had to cling to.'

'Simon,' she whispered, 'please stop...'

'That's almost as good,' he murmured, then looked up ruefully as the stewardess appeared at his side offering drinks. 'Uh—thanks,' he said to her. 'I think my wife and I deserve some champagne.'

From the airport they caught the Gatwick Express and then got a taxi from Victoria Station straight to

Madame's house. It was a Sunday and Simon said, 'We might as well get this over and done with.'

'You're *what*?'

'Married, Yvette,' he repeated amusedly. 'And before you say any more, who was it who told Martha all sorts of lies and sent her almost directly to Mull?'

'Sit down,' Madame said, tottering towards a chair herself. 'This 'as taken me a leetle by surprise.' But when she had almost lowered herself into the chair, she shot upright again, advanced upon Martha and enveloped her in her arms, saying, 'So I was right. I knew it!' This was said gleefully. 'Did I not tell you what an expert I am at reading the 'uman 'eart? Oh, I am so 'appy for you! And what do a few white lies mean when the end result is so—stunning? Tell me this, Martha Winters!'

'Martha Macquarie,' Simon murmured.

'Martha Macquarie,' Madame said grandly. 'Does she not look stunning too, Simon?'

'I have to agree with you entirely.'

'If I may be allowed to say a word...'

Martha stopped and blinked suddenly, whereupon Madame hugged her again, chuckled, said, 'New brides can get a bit tearful—do we not all know it?' and then commanded Simon to break out a bottle of her best champagne.

She was to say later, 'My only regret—what did you wear, Martha?'

Simon reached for Martha's hand. 'I told you.' He turned to his aunt. 'She bought a dress in Edinburgh.'

Madame wrinkled her nose.

'A dress that nearly bowled me over,' he added wryly, 'with her in it.'

'Ah, well—there's always one that gets away.' Madame shrugged philosophically, then she regarded Simon narrowly and said with all the lack of delicacy she was capable of, 'I trust you do not plan to whisk her straight into purdah, Simon. I've fashioned a whole new collection around her. This could be a disaster now I come to think of it!'

They both laughed at her comically horrified expression and it was Martha who said, 'We've agreed that I should work a bit longer if you'd like me to.'

'*Like* you to——'

'But not full-time, Yvette,' Simon broke in. 'And not out of town.'

A snapping black gaze intercepted a suddenly cool, firm grey-green one but it was Madame who relented. 'Very well,' she said, with injured dignity.

But Simon merely said placidly, 'Tell us about Bahrain—talking of purdah.'

'So this is where you live.'

Martha looked round another elegant Chelsea house, this one looking on to Onslow Square.

'This is where I live—when I'm not living elsewhere,' he said with a slight grimace. 'But it's never felt as much a home as Mull.'

'It's lovely, though,' she said, then frowned faintly as it struck a chord in her mind, something to do with the mixture of delicate colours.

'It's all Yvette's doing——'

'Of course!' she broke in. 'I couldn't quite place what was familiar about it. She has this unerring eye for colours, doesn't she?' And she gazed around at the mix of off-white walls, magnolia carpet and curtains, and straw-coloured chairs and settees with pale jade touches in lampshades and cushions. 'You and Yvette are quite close, aren't you?' she added as the thought struck her.

'We are,' he agreed. 'When we're not in total discord. I think it has something to do with us being the last bastion of the Macquaries, even if it is only by marriage in her case—well, to date, that is. But she certainly threw herself heart and soul in with us when she married my uncle—she often acts more Macquarie than the real thing. And she takes an inordinate interest in my affairs, as we both know,' he said a shade drily, 'probably as a result of not being able to provide an heir to the name herself.'

'But you're fond of her all the same,' Martha said.

'Yes, I'm fond of her.' He came to stand right in front of her. 'I can't wait to show you what she did to the main bedroom.'

'You don't have to wait.'

'Thank you,' he said gravely. 'I thought I might have scared you off with what I said on the plane.'

Martha considered this then said equally gravely, 'You might have, on the plane. This could be different.'

'Tell me more,' he murmured.

She drew a breath, amazed at the flood of longing that filled her as he stood before her, tall and casual in the jeans, open-necked shirt and tweed jacket he'd travelled in, not dissimilar to her outfit of jeans, white blouse and navy blue blazer.

'Martha?'

Her lips moved once, then she said huskily as she reached for his hand and placed it on her heart, 'I guess . . . it's lovely to be on our own again.'

He swept her into his arms . . .

'Where are you going?' he said lazily a lot later, and stopped her from leaving the bed.

Martha smiled down at him. 'To fulfil my usual role—to make us something to eat. It's way past dinnertime.'

'Glory be,' he marvelled, and pulled her back down beside him to run his hands over her body. 'Nearly an entire afternoon and early evening spent doing this. We could get into the *Guinness Book of Records*.'

'I doubt it—we've also slept,' she pointed out a little wickedly.

'We could do it once more—and sleep again,' he said against her breasts. 'What's the point of having a bedroom like this if you don't honour its obvious intentions?'

Martha grimaced and glanced around as she ran her fingers through his hair. For it was an unashamedly sensual bedroom. High above the bed a cupid on the wall held up a draped canopy of peach silk that was echoed in matching silk sheets with an ivory lace trim and a sumptuous padded peach silk bedspread, while the rest of the room was all ivory and gold. There was even an ivory carpet that flowed through to the *en-suite* bathroom, ivory tiles, gold fittings and triple gold-rimmed mirrors. 'Its intentions are certainly obvious, I have to agree with you,' she said, 'but peach and ivory are very flattering to one's skin.'

'Ah!' He lifted his head and looked into her eyes. 'So that accounts for it.'

'What?' she said innocently.

'Why I have not the slightest desire to get up out of this bed. Your skin——' he drew a finger down the curve of her hip '—is quite soft and peachy enough without any flattery. I might have to remove us to a monastery,' he said reflectively, but added, 'Seriously, are you telling me that now you've had your way with me and reduced me to this you're going to get up and walk away?'

'Seriously, yes.'

His lips quirked. 'Then all I can say is yes, ma'am; thank you, ma'am.' But the way his eyes glinted told a different story and his hands stayed on her body.

Thus it was that it was about half an hour later before Martha did leave the bed after a short, sweet interlude, which he'd concluded this time by saying, 'There—sorry about that but I just couldn't help myself. You're free to do whatever you like now.'

She said, but with a smile in her eyes, 'You're impossible sometimes, Simon Macquarie.'

'It's what you do to me, Martha,' he replied, kissing her then lying back with his head on his arm. 'Don't lose sight of that, will you?'

She said on a suddenly indrawn breath, 'I won't. Hungry?'

'Mmm,' he said ruefully. And she bent down and returned his kiss lightly then got up.

But by the time she'd showered and put on pyjamas and an ivory towelling gown that came with the room she saw that he'd fallen asleep. And she stood looking down at him with her heart in her eyes for a moment, then drew the sheet up gently and turned away.

She discovered the kitchen in the basement after inspecting the house from top to bottom and detecting Yvette's hand almost everywhere: in three other bedrooms, the library and dining-room, and even the kitchen, which had a decidedly French flavour to its décor, with hanging copper pots, a free-standing chopping-block, a rack of excellent knives and the general kind of practicality the French gave to their cooking. But there was one room that appeared to have escaped Yvette—a bedroom on the second floor that was luxurious but simple—no looped, draped curtains here, no delicate pastels, very much a man's room in fact, despite the double bed. And upon further inspection she realised it was Simon's bedroom with all his clothes in it, which led her to wonder if he'd ever used the peach room, unless... No, don't even wonder about it, she chided herself.

There was a note on the fridge from his cleaning lady saying she'd brought in fresh bread, milk and eggs as requested, plus a cooked chicken and some salad ingredients. He must have rung her from France, Martha thought, and she looked around the practical kitchen with a sudden gleam in her eye. The truth was she did enjoy cooking; she even found it soothing—not that she needed to be soothed... or did she?

Surely not, she told herself, and unhooked a frying-pan, adding firmly, No, I don't. But as she found some onions, capsicum and mushrooms and set about chopping them an insidious little spring of tension did dissolve within her...

She also found a packet of rice and set some to cook while she sautéd the vegetables lightly in olive oil, added an improvised stock and then chicken pieces from the cooked cold bird, thus creating a fricassee. She made a salad and popped the rolls in the oven to warm and had just set the kitchen table with a red checked cloth she'd found when a sound at the doorway disturbed her.

It was Simon, wearing his jeans and an old football jersey with its collar askew. Simon with his hair unbrushed and his eyes still sleepy, watching her from the doorway with his shoulders propped against it, his arms folded.

She smiled wryly. 'I was just wondering whether to wake you.'

He said nothing for a moment, his eyes roaming up and down her, still clad in the dressing-gown but with a butcher's apron over it, her hair tied back in a simple ponytail. Then he sniffed appreciatively. 'I've a feeling you're going to make a gem of a wife, Martha,' he murmured. 'How on earth did you come up with this?'

She told him and invited him to sit down. And they shared a companionable meal, talking idly until all of a sudden Martha ran out of energy and slight shadows appeared under her eyes. She said, 'Sorry—I haven't even done the dishes.'

He smiled slightly and, taking her hand, helped her to her feet. 'I'll do them—but I'll take you up to bed first. No, don't argue, Martha,' he said.

So she went with him but he paused outside the peach bedroom then turned her towards his own and when she looked at him questioningly he said, 'This bed is freshly made up. It'll be more comfortable.'

It was, too, she found, after he helped her take her dressing-gown off and she slid down between cool, crisp cotton sheets. 'Will you...?' She didn't finish her question, biting her lip awkwardly instead.

'Will I come and sleep with you? Of course,' he said quietly, sitting down on the edge of the bed and examining those faint shadows beneath her eyes then smiling, but strangely unamusedly. 'You look so young with no make-up and your hair like that.'

She yawned behind her fingers and said huskily, 'I don't know why but I feel rather young at the moment.'

'Perhaps I've been overdoing it,' he commented after a moment.

'I didn't mean that.'

'No, but all the same...' He paused. 'I have to go back to work tomorrow—will you mind?'

'If you have to—that's an awkward question, Simon.'

He grinned fleetingly. 'Sorry. I do have to, unfortunately. Whereas you aren't starting back with Yvette on a limited basis until next week; but I thought it would give you time to get to know the house, make any changes

you'd like to, get to know my cleaning lady and reor-
ganise her if you want to, et cetera.'

'I don't think I'll be changing anything.'

'Martha——' he narrowed his eyes '—it's your house
now. And I'll be opening a bank account in your name
tomorrow as well as finding you a car——'

He stopped as she sat up suddenly, looking distressed.
'What's wrong?'

'I've got money of my own,' she whispered.

'Not enough to run this place,' he pointed out. 'Or
are you trying to tell me you object to me keeping you?'

She sank back, looking confused.

'Martha?'

'I suppose I hadn't thought about it yet. I...'

'It's the way most marriages work,' he said, with a
tinge of irony, she thought. 'But, if it bothers you, were
I suddenly to become destitute,' he added, in a different
tone, 'you could keep me.'

She had to smile.

'Go to sleep now and stop worrying,' he said, and
took her left hand and raised it to his lips. But he stopped
suddenly and frowned and fiddled with her wedding-
ring, which was a fraction too big but they hadn't had
time to get it altered. 'Look, give this to me tomorrow
morning together with your engagement ring to get the
size right. I know a good jeweller.' He lifted her hand
again and kissed it. 'Goodnight, my dear,' he said gently.
'Sweet dreams.'

Two days later Martha made herself a cup of tea in the
kitchen and sat down at the table with it. She'd just had
an exhausting session with the voluble cleaning lady
Simon employed and come to realise just how much was
involved in maintaining a house of this size.

So, she thought, am I up to it? She looked around a little dazedly with her cup held in both hands then jumped as the doorbell pealed. She glanced ruefully down at her tracksuit bottoms, deck shoes and baggy sweater, then went to answer it as it pealed impatiently again.

It was Sondra Grant.

CHAPTER EIGHT

THEY stared at each other then Sondra said in a low, overwrought voice, 'I knew it—I knew he had someone with him and it had to be you. Well, I tried to be sensible and rational about it all, but now I'm going to tell you a few home truths before it's too late and we all get hurt. Martha, let me in!'

'Sondra——'

'No, you owe me one, Martha,' the other girl said determinedly and simply pushed past her.

Martha closed the front door after hesitating briefly, but it was pouring and Sondra had already divested herself of her raincoat, hung it up and, under her dazed gaze, started down the staircase towards the kitchen.

'Sondra...' she attempted again when they arrived in the kitchen, but after taking a look at her strained white face she said quietly, 'I've just made some tea. Would you like some?'

'Why not?' Sondra responded bitterly. 'You've certainly made yourself at home. Do you know that I *never* spent a night in this house? And do you know why? Because he's kept it like a shrine to Morag.' She laughed harshly. 'Yvette did it up for them as a wedding-present. But here's the interesting thing. Do you know why *you're* here? Because you couldn't be more different from her if you tried,' she said contemptuously. 'I know, we were friends. He doesn't love you, Martha. It's just that he can't bear to be reminded of her.'

'Is that so?' Martha pushed a cup of tea towards her. 'Drink some,' she advised. 'Or would you like a brandy instead?'

'I'd love a brandy,' Sondra said hollowly but unfortunately after Martha had got her one it seemed to give her new fire. 'That's why I came to tell you——' she swallowed another sip '—it would be a disaster for you to read more into it than there is, Martha. I came to tell you that *no one* can give him what they had, but at least I can give him some peace and understanding and love. Oh, you're beautiful enough, but next to her no one would even have noticed; she fascinated everyone.'

Martha stared down at her ringless left hand on the table and thought, She doesn't know. What do I do now? She got up and poured herself a brandy. 'Why shouldn't I be able to do that?' she said huskily as the moment stretched. 'Give him some peace and—love.'

'Because you don't understand,' Sondra said bitterly. 'You never saw them together; you don't really know him——'

'Sondra——' Martha swung round suddenly '—I knew him three years ago——'

'For a few weeks on the other side of the world,' Sondra said scathingly. 'And that was after Morag, anyway!'

'All the same, we came to know each other quite well.'

'I can imagine!' There was insolence in Sondra's dark eyes now as she added, 'Did you manage to hold him? Of course not. Mind you, you got a bit cleverer when you rolled up here, didn't you? All that standing him up and walking out on him—what an act!'

Martha took a deep breath. 'It wasn't as a matter of fact. Sondra, I don't quite know how to tell you this, and I hope that one day you'll forgive me, but—we're married now.'

'What?' Sondra said blankly.

'Yes. My rings are at the jewellers; one of them was a bit big. Look, I'm sorry,' she said helplessly.

'Oh, my God—what have I done?' Sondra whispered, and put the back of her hand to her mouth.

'You haven't told me anything I didn't already know,' Martha said quietly. 'Except one thing. Did you—did Simon lead you to believe he would marry you?'

Sondra stared at her out of agonised eyes, then dropped her head on to the table and started to cry. 'No. He did the opposite,' she sobbed. 'But I persisted and...I really thought I was winning him over until he came to me a few weeks back and said he had to end it. But he also told me——' she raised her blotchy, tear-streaked face at last '—it wasn't so he could go to you.'

Martha moved her shoulders and took her first sip of brandy. 'I think he meant that at the time. We didn't expect to run into each other the way we did.'

'I wonder,' Sondra said, and stood up abruptly. 'I've got to go. How long have you been married?'

Martha bit her lip. 'Just over a week.'

'Here we are,' Simon said at dinner that night, and drew a box containing her rings from his pocket. 'Try them now.'

So she slid her wedding-ring on and it fitted perfectly. She then pushed the beautiful pear-shaped diamond on in front of it and looked down at them with her mind in turmoil—as it had been ever since Sondra's visit. Then she made a decision and smiled faintly across at him. 'Thanks, that's much better. I had a visitor today.'

Simon raised an eyebrow. 'Most people I know are out of London at the moment, on holiday.'

'This one wasn't.' Martha started to serve the paella she'd made.

'So? Why the reserve and restraint?' He was frowning at her now.

'Because it was all a bit... it was Sondra.'

He was quite still for a moment, then, 'I see.'

Martha sat down. 'I'm only telling you because if you run into her it's bound to come out—and you're probably bound to run into her in the course of business if nothing else.'

'Go on—by the way, she is officially on holiday at the moment too. Did she tell you that?'

'No. But I had to tell her we were married.'

'Did she accuse you of stealing me?'

Martha glanced across the table and discovered he was watching her with an austere, set expression. 'Look, it's over,' she said slowly. 'So...'

'No, it's not,' he countered roughly, 'if it's going to lie like a sort of poison on your mind. What did she say?'

A little spark of anger lit in Martha's heart. 'That's between the two of us, Simon,' she said coolly. 'And that's how it's going to stay.'

'Don't tell me you still feel guilty about Sondra?' he queried with an arrogant lift of an eyebrow.

'If anyone should,' Martha replied through her teeth, 'it's not me.'

'You mean I should?'

'*Yes*,' she said, but more because of his attitude, she realised immediately, than because she believed it entirely.

'So she did inject a little poison,' he said softly. 'It didn't take much to make you into a disbeliever, Martha.' And his grey-green gaze raked her.

Martha breathed distraughtly. 'Why are you taking it like this?' she said incredulously. 'I'm the one who should be upset, I'm the one she told you've kept this house like a shrine to——' She stopped abruptly and stood up convulsively, knocking her chair over as he smiled a brief, unamused smile of victory.

But he was also up in a flash and he'd got to her before she reached the door and pinned her arms to her sides. 'Don't fight me, Martha,' he warned grimly. 'You'll only get hurt. I would never do anything so ridiculous as to keep a house as a shrine to anyone.'

'But you didn't bring Sondra here,' she panted, still struggling despite his warning.

'She told you that too? No, I didn't—but what she may have neglected to tell you is that, despite her allusions and so on, our affair—if you could call it that— was never consummated.'

Martha gasped. 'I don't believe you...'

'Believe what you like; it's true.'

'So...' Martha sagged in his arms then recovered. 'But why did you let me think it was?'

'I was, believe it or not,' he said grimly again, 'trying to save her pride. It was a little difficult to contradict her in front of her—— Oh, hell,' he said wearily. 'Look, can you sit down and listen to the truth about Sondra now?

'I've known her for years,' he said after getting Martha a glass of wine and holding her hand around it while she took a few sips. 'She was a friend of Morag's, we moved in the same crowd, then she got her degree and started to work with the firm of auditors that do our books and was eventually assigned to our account. That was when we began to see more of each other; I suppose it started about a year ago, but quite slowly—contact in the office stretching to contact after work and not just with a group of people we both knew. Dinners, theatres and things like that,' he said broodingly. 'And almost imperceptibly it drifted on to being invited out as a couple, doing things as a couple—some things.

'To be honest——' he raised his eyes to Martha's suddenly '—I wondered at her patience sometimes, when I made no further moves, but it suited me, which is something I don't take a great deal of pride in.' He shrugged. 'But, you see, I also began to wonder if Sondra mightn't be the answer for me.'

There was a taut, electric little pause before he went on, 'Then you walked back into my life and I knew that it couldn't be. Unfortunately, I also belatedly woke up to the fact that Sondra, despite treading so carefully, despite presenting to *me* a sort of adult, very much career-woman image that I'd assumed was a lot tougher than it is, was nurturing great hopes,' he said flatly. 'And not only that—her pride was involved.'

'So you told her when you broke it off that it wasn't because of me?' Martha whispered.

'No. Not exactly. She accused me of breaking it off so that I could rush away into your arms. I said to her that the likelihood of that was nil, which, while not untrue at the time, was, I admit, a slightly evasive way of putting things, and more so as things have turned out. Should I feel guilty about Sondra?' he added abruptly. 'Yes, you're right, I should, which is probably why I didn't explain this to you sooner. But how would you have recommended me to handle it, Martha? Should I have walked away and never said a word?'

'I...' Martha took a shuddering breath. 'No. I'm sorry but so much has happened to me and when people keep *telling* me about Morag, how you'll never forget her——'

'Martha——' he took her hand '—that's what Sondra told me too but she had no idea...' He paused. 'That's something she can't know, and nor can anyone else, only you and I. I suppose——' for a moment his eyes were so bleak that Martha shivered '—the fact that I haven't told you I love you more than I ever loved Morag is responsible for the way you feel. Believe me, I wish I could, Martha.' He stopped and cupped her face gently. 'But——' and for a moment the bleakness in his eyes turned to a kind of torture '—the truth is I don't have much faith in eternal declarations of love and I'd much rather we lived it than talked about it.'

She moistened her lips and wondered if this was his way of telling her at last that he could never love anyone the way he'd loved Morag. At least now I know, she thought, perhaps I can cope with it...

But he said abruptly, 'I should never have done it,' and withdrew his hands.

'Married me?' she said huskily as she came to a quiet, painful but oddly peaceful decision. 'I don't regret it.' And she picked up his wrist and kissed the inside of it lingeringly for a moment. Then she blinked and said with a wry little smile, 'Is this another dinner we're going to wreck?'

In the event, they did. Because he took her up to bed there and then, made achingly beautiful love to her and held her in his arms until she fell asleep.

She got another visitor the next morning but this time a more joyful one.

'Annabel!' she gasped as she opened the door and then they fell into each other's arms.

'But how did you know I'd be here?' she queried when they were drinking coffee, comfortably installed in the kitchen.

Annabel put her mug down and said reproachfully, 'Not from you!'

'I know.' Martha twisted her rings awkwardly. 'It all happened in a bit of a rush.'

Annabel chuckled. 'So I gather! But Simon rang me. He said I'd probably like to know about it before I read it in *The Times*—it's due to appear tomorrow. Now tell me all about it, Martha!' she commanded.

So Martha attempted to do so although she left out more than she put in, and the other girl proved that she was both a wise and genuine friend by not probing any further but settling down instead to impart her own news. 'I'm going to Scone,' she said dramatically.

'Scone—in Australia?'

'The same,' Annabel said with satisfaction. 'Paul has invited me out when he goes home in a couple of months' time. I think it's a sort of presenting me to his parents expedition. I've done the same.'

'And they've approved—is it that serious now?'

Annabel grimaced. 'They do like him but they'd much rather I married closer to home. Still, they have four other daughters to hand to vent their maternal and paternal feelings on and there's always Ricky. And yes, although marriage hasn't been mentioned, we're pretty serious about each other. Funnily enough, despite being so gorgeous and dashing on a polo field, Paul is a *very* serious person who doesn't rush into things. Mind you, he hasn't the slightest hope of getting away from me; he just doesn't know it yet.'

Martha had to giggle then they were both laughing together until Martha said, 'I hope Ricky isn't—well, he's probably got someone else by now anyway.'

'Ricky will be demolished,' Annabel said cheerfully, causing Martha to wince, 'but only for a few weeks. He's far too young to think about getting married anyway and I always told him you weren't for him.'

'Thanks—I don't know whether to be offended or otherwise,' Martha said ruefully. 'Not that I didn't tell him that myself, but I liked him all the same.'

'Darling,' Annabel said gently, 'it was always obvious that what was between you and Simon was way out of the boys' league, which Ricky is still very obviously in.'

Martha said involuntarily, 'I sometimes wish I were still in a similar league.' She bit her lip but it was too late.

'Let me guess,' Annabel said quietly. 'There are some ghosts that are hard to lay? No, don't talk about it if you don't want to, but funnily enough I was one of the few people who didn't like Morag, nor, when everyone was saying how different you were, did I ever read anything into it on Simon's behalf. In fact it was just that which started to annoy me and made me determined to get to know you.'

'Thanks,' Martha said huskily.

'Well! Seeing as you're a lady of leisure entirely this week, why don't we go out to lunch tomorrow? Why don't we get really tarted up and go somewhere where all the right people will see us—well, as many as we can muster at this time of the year—and I'll be able to show off my good friend Mrs Martha Macquarie?'

'I...' Martha hesitated.

'Martha, one last thing before we close this topic,' Annabel said gently. 'There are some ghosts only you can lay—and that includes Sondra.'

'I... Perhaps you're right. Thanks again,' Martha replied.

'I got trapped into a bit of a shopping spree today,' Martha said the next evening. It had been a glorious summer day and Simon had rung from work to suggest that they go out for dinner and so she was beside him in the Jaguar, which Picton had returned from Scotland, as they drove to an open-air restaurant where he said the food was excellent.

'I thought I hadn't seen that dress before,' he said with a lurking little smile. 'I hope you allowed me to pay for it.'

Martha looked downwards ruefully. The dress was a ribbed, knitted oatmeal tube with short sleeves, a short skirt and a scooped neckline. She wore a string of chunky amber beads with it, and her hair was put up loosely. 'An inordinate amount as it happens for what little there is of it.'

'You look sensational, however. What else were you lured into buying?'

'I wouldn't say that—I didn't take much luring, to be honest—but I was unwise enough to admit to Annabel that I hadn't got a trousseau. So she took me to this marvellous lingerie shop.'

Simon groaned.

'But I spent my own money on that,' Martha said impishly.

'That wasn't what I meant,' he murmured with a wicked little smile and put his hand over hers. 'Am I to expect you to wear something infinitely sexy to bed tonight?'

'I'm wearing some pretty sexy new underwear at the moment,' she said seriously, then laughed at his expression. 'Just teasing. No, none of it's particularly sexy, just lovely fabrics and lace and tucks and things. Perhaps we should discontinue this conversation,' she added as his hand moved from hers to her thigh where the short dress ended.

'In case we both start to look anorexic because we've wrecked so many dinners? I agree with you entirely,' he said gravely but didn't withdraw his hand.

'Well, I didn't mean to be provocative,' Martha said as the thought suddenly occurred to her, and blushed.

He did take his hand away then but to touch her lightly on the cheek before he gave his whole attention back to his driving. 'I don't think there's anything wrong with a husband and wife discussing underwear, but I'll tell you something else.' He waited until she turned to him, still looking faintly embarrassed. 'I'm still very much enjoying a wife who can be made to blush.'

Martha grimaced, but it went on to be a warm, light-hearted evening. She told him how well she was getting on with his cleaning lady, how nice it was to have a friend like Annabel, how she missed Yvette and was looking forward to going back to work on a limited basis. 'I don't think I could sit at home *all* day,' she said thoughtfully, 'but it's rather nice to have a home to think about.'

'I'm glad,' he said simply. They'd finished their meal and he was leaning back in his chair watching her idly. 'I'm only sorry that we couldn't have had a longer honeymoon, but that doesn't mean to say we can't have a second one.'

Martha propped her chin on her hands. 'Tell me more about work—you did say you were off to Japan shortly.'

His look was wry. 'I sent someone else. We were actually getting married on the day I was due to leave. Work?' he mused. 'Well, you saw the distillery at Cognac but I operate mostly from our offices in London, although we have them in Bordeaux and Edinburgh too. There are a few other companies in the group now, wineries et cetera, and we've just bought a pottery, which is why I'm so busy at the moment. As a matter of fact...' he paused ' ... you could find that interesting, Martha, since you're keen on art and ceramics. I'll take you over there the first free day I get.'

'Thanks!' she said enthusiastically, feeling a warm little glow.

They drove home not long afterwards and while he checked the fax machine she went upstairs to get ready for bed, putting on one of her beautiful new nightgowns. She'd just slid it over her head when she turned at a sound in the doorway and saw him standing there watching her. He'd discarded his jacket, unbuttoned his collar and unknotted his tie, which was still hanging loosely around his neck. He waited a moment, his gaze roaming over the confection of white broderie anglaise with narrow black ribbons threaded through the neck and hemline that had drifted down her body, before he said, 'It's lovely, but unfortunately what you just did is about to be reversed.'

Martha trembled at the naked desire in his eyes but tried to keep her head and said, 'I probably won't mind.'

He smiled slightly. 'Such an accommodating wife, too. Come here.'

She went. But before he touched her he said, 'Is it getting easier—being married to me?'

She looked up into his eyes. 'Yes.'

But as the golden summer started to slide into autumn it—albeit almost imperceptibly at first—started to go wrong.

For one thing Simon turned out to be, she believed, a compulsive worker. And when she teased him about it once and said wryly that she'd love to be able to take him away where there'd be no work for a whole year, for a moment she thought she saw that darkness come back to his expression. In fact she got the feeling—she couldn't say why but nevertheless couldn't shake it— that that was when things did start to go downhill. She couldn't say why, because it wasn't as if their love life was any different—it was still sometimes electric, sometimes tender and sweet, and always her haven to lie beside

him or wake up beside him and feel the reassurance of
his arms around her or his body next to hers. Which,
she discovered more and more, she needed as lonely days
succeeded lonely days, lonely despite working for Yvette
but only on a part-time basis. Nor did he go away on
any trips, which she wondered about, until she got in-
fluenza and wasn't able to accompany him to New
York...

He was only away for five days but insisted on flying
Grace down from Mull to look after her and Yvette called
in daily.

'I really don't need all this,' Martha said to her thickly
once. 'I'm quite capable of having flu on my own.'

'You should never look a gift horse in the mouth,'
Yvette said sternly. 'Besides which, I don't think 'e likes
to think of you rattling around 'ere on your own. By
the way, do you like what I did to 'is 'ouse? I've meant
to ask you a couple of times.'

'Very much—Yvette, why didn't you ever tell me about
Morag, even when you were pushing me at Simon? You
must have known why the gossips were having such a
field day—because I'm so different.' She grimaced.

'*Chérie*,' Yvette said simply. 'Morag or no Morag,
from the moment you only restrained yourself by a 'air's
breadth from dashing a glass of sherry into 'is face, I
knew you were the one for him.'

Martha had to smile, then had to blow her nose furiously, but Yvette went on in a curiously cautious manner,
'He 'as not made you aware of this yet?'

'He has. I just wonder sometimes, that's all.'

'Well, don't be such a silly girl! Now, let me show you
these designs. You can tell me what you think quite
honestly.'

'I think,' Martha said slowly some minutes later, 'that
Simon was right—all they lack are a yashmak or two.

But,' she added with a wicked little grin as Yvette started to swell, 'They're sensational!'

Madame subsided then she said a strange thing. She said, 'You know, I like you so much better than I ever liked Morag.'

That's two people, Martha thought that night. Yet Grace obviously liked her. Strange...

The day Simon was due home he rang her to explain that he'd been delayed and would be away for another four days. She took a breath and suggested she fly over since she was feeling so much better and had even sent Grace home to Scotland. He hesitated, then, sounding curiously strained and tired, said, No, he was going to be so busy it wouldn't be any fun for her, and certainly no kind of convalescence.

She put the phone down wistfully, decided the house felt a bit like a prison and took herself off to see Yvette at work, where she was press-ganged into trying on some of the new designs. In the middle of this, someone came into the shop and requested to see some clothes, and after Yvette had been assured by the assistant that the two women looked rich enough to buy the Ritz she asked Martha if she'd mind modelling them. So Yvette took Martha to the reception-room where the two women sat drinking coffee from a Sèvres set, but stopped on the threshold so abruptly that Martha, wearing a glorious caftan but with protestations that she didn't look her best only just dying on her lips, nearly bumped into her.

Then Yvette moved forward and said in a cold voice, 'Ah, Iris. We meet again.'

An exceptionally well-groomed, exquisitely dressed, middle-aged woman turned to the doorway and replied equally coolly, 'So we do, Yvette,' before her eyes flicked beyond Yvette and came to rest on Martha. 'Are you going to introduce me? Never mind, I'll do it myself,' she murmured, and stood up. 'You must be Martha; this is my daughter-in-law-to-be, Fiona, but you probably know of *me* better because of my daughter—Morag.'

Martha, who'd been about to extend her hand, found her gaze flying to Yvette instead and for a moment one could have heard—literally, given the circumstances—a pin drop.

Then Iris continued smoothly, 'Fiona is putting together a trousseau, Yvette, and since your clothes have become such a rage around town and she was determined to have some I thought, Why not?' She shrugged elegantly. 'I did wonder if I'd bump into Simon's new bride at the same time—dear me, there is no likeness at all, is there?'

'No, none,' Yvette said, and Martha, blinking, realised she was talking through clenched teeth. 'On the contrary,' Yvette continued, 'I don't think two girls could be more dissimilar.'

Morag's mother, Martha saw, had yellowy hazel eyes and at that moment she also saw an expression of almost vicious anger pass through them before Iris said smoothly, 'Well, but didn't it amuse you, Yvette? The way no one was—er—brave enough to come out and say, Is Simon Macquarie trying to replace Morag Wallace in his life with someone who will never remind him of her?'

Yvette strolled further into the room. 'No, it didn't amuse me, Iris, because, you see, it just isn't true. Now, my dear Fiona——' she turned her attention to the girl of about twenty-two, still sitting in one of the gold chairs with a startled look in her eyes '—if you would really like some of my clothes for your trousseau, come and see me on your own. *Au revoir*, ladies,' she added. 'My *vendeuse* will show you out.' And she forcibly propelled Martha out of the room ahead of her.

'What——'

'Take no notice, Martha,' Yvette commanded. 'I am in such a rage I could keel quite easily, but take no notice.'

'How *can* I?' Martha demanded, and didn't realise how pale she looked.

'Where is Simon?' Yvette sat down and pulled the phone towards her.

'He's in New York, as you very well know, but——'

'Then I will get him in New York—this 'as gone on long enough.'

'What—will you please tell me *what* has gone on long enough? Look, do you think I don't know how much he loved her?' Martha said, and put her hands to her face abruptly. 'Do you think I need her mother to tell me that? Everyone tells me.'

'Did *I* ever tell you this?' Yvette broke off and spoke into the phone, apparently to Simon's secretary, then finally banged the phone down. 'He can't be got hold of at the moment—foolish girl! Does she think I can be put off?'

'Please,' Martha said, 'don't do this—there's no *need*. Madame,' she added dangerously, 'I swear I'll never talk to you again if you bother Simon like this.'

They glared at each other until Yvette said, 'And what are *you* going to do?'

'Nothing. What do you expect me to do?'

'You did once pack your bags and tell me there was no place on earth like Australia and you couldn't imagine why you'd ever left it. Come and have dinner with me and Oswald tonight; we 'ave a few people coming, but if you like I'll put them off. Yes——'

'No.' Martha made herself smile as she added, 'Don't you dare do that either. In fact Annabel is coming to have dinner with me,' she said, quite fictitiously but desperate to defuse the situation. 'As for Australia, do you know she's fallen in love with one of us?'

Yvette stared at her then smiled reluctantly herself at last. 'It must be catching.'

But in the end the lonely house got to Martha.

To make matters worse, she'd just got a letter from Jane, whom she'd kept in touch with, exclaiming enthusiastically over Martha's marriage and imparting the news of her own. There was no mistaking her joy both for Martha and herself. And the photo she'd enclosed of her wedding had shown two people radiantly in love.

Martha found herself wandering around the house with the photo in her hand until she took herself to task and commanded herself to think objectively about the last month—the first month of her marriage. Think objectively for the first time perhaps, sitting on the staircase hugging her knees. And in her heart of hearts she had to admit that she should have given a lot more thought to marrying Simon Macquarie at the same time as she acknowledged that he'd brought the most powerful pressure to bear on her. *That's* got to mean something, hasn't it? she told herself, but then out of the blue she remembered something her mother had once told her, something she'd read somewhere, she'd said, that went something along the lines of you never could tell with men, even the best of them...

The faintest smile touched her lips but she sobered almost immediately and thought, Well, assuming that's true, he didn't *have* to marry me to get me into bed. But assuming the opposite is true, and because of the physical attraction, because he'd decided to marry anyway—did he really know what he was getting other than someone who wouldn't remind him of Morag? Do I know yet what kind of a wife Martha Winters will be...?

She stirred then as this seemed to touch the heart of her dilemma. Not altogether the poised, sophisticated creature I might have assumed I was, she confessed to herself. Could that be the problem? I seem to have gone from an angry young woman to a quiet, even uncertain one, desperate for reassurance and even burying myself in my home for comfort... Am I shrivelling because of a continual awareness—not to mention the way people are always *reminding* me—of how different I am from Morag?

She grimaced and stroked the banister while she admitted as well that even in her uncertainty she was a very domesticated wife, taking more and more pride in her home... because it seemed so long since she'd had a home, and never one of her own, to be the complete mistress of? she asked herself. But why, if he doesn't want me to be any other kind of wife, should he object to that? she wondered. And why is my life like this after what he said anyway? It didn't sound as if it was going to be this way at the time. Could he be waiting for me to say I'd like to start a family so I could be shunted off to Mull and we'd have that kind of life—me up there occupied with children and the estate and he coming and going? How would I feel about that?

She stared into space for a long time then got up suddenly and decided to go to the movies before she thought any more and talked herself into believing that Simon was regretting their marriage.

She ended up watching a double feature and getting home late, then remembering early the next morning that it was the cleaning lady's day off and that she'd promised to go riding with Annabel and Paul. So she left the house early after making it as neat as a new pin, not hard with just herself in it, and ended up spending the whole day with them at a show-jumping event.

It was about six in the evening when she let herself back in, feeling tired, but quite pleasantly so, and certainly in a more positive frame of mind—to find Simon apparently waiting for her, his eyes as cold as ice.

He said grimly, 'Where the bloody hell have you been, Martha?'

CHAPTER NINE

SIMON was wearing a dark suit, a blue silk shirt and a grey and navy tie and he looked every inch a powerful, influential man who was very used to getting his own way. In fact, the slightest resemblance to the man who'd fished with her in tattered clothes, the man who sometimes roamed around the house in bare feet, jeans and an old football jersey and made love to her sometimes with laughter and an achingly gentle touch threaded through the sensuality was no longer there, Martha discovered, and although she discovered it with a jolt of pain she felt a spark of anger ignite...

'Where should I be?' she countered, and tossed her head. 'You surely don't expect me to sit at home all the time you're away?'

He said through his teeth, 'I expect you to be home at midnight, though. Is that such an unreal expectation to have of a wife?'

Martha narrowed her eyes. 'What are you saying, Simon? That you don't trust me?'

'Well, I won't know that, will I, Martha, until you tell me where you were when I rang at intervals all through the evening last night until midnight—at which time I boarded a flight to bring me home?' he said. 'But you weren't home when I arrived either. Was Annabel coming to have dinner with you an invention, but one that was in the family?' he added roughly.

'How did you know about that?' Martha whispered, colouring a little as she thought of the lie she'd told

166

Yvette, then beginning to understand—but too late, it seemed. 'So she did ring you?'

'Yvette? She rang me,' he agreed. 'She told me you were distraught after meeting Morag's mother. That's why I'm here, but it seems she was wrong, doesn't it, Martha?' he said, with a look up and down her that was patently arrogant and insolent.

Martha took a breath, and cracked. 'I've just... I've had enough,' she stated. 'Where would you like to think I was, Simon? With another man? OK, you pick one— but of course, how dumb of me,' she marvelled. 'I missed the crack about being in the family—you thought I was with Ricky, didn't you? Why not?'

'Don't play games with me, Martha,' he warned savagely. 'Just tell me where you were.'

'No,' she said hoarsely, white to the lips but her eyes a dark, angry blue.

He took a menacing step towards her.

'And you can't make me either,' she added defiantly.

'We'll see,' he said through his teeth. 'Incidentally, when I'm tired of this marriage, I'll let you know, but until then we'll go on as before.'

'No,' she breathed. 'Oh, no, we won't, and if you think you're going to force anything out of me, Simon——' she said incredulously, and stopped as he loomed over her.

'Force it out of you—no,' he said almost gently. 'But we might just put something to the test—does Ricky make you feel the way I do?'

'Simon,' she whispered as he drew her into his arms, 'that's not fair...'

'Isn't it? Don't you know what they say about love and war?' He studied the outline of her mouth from beneath half-closed lids then bent his head to kiss her.

She tried to fight him but he picked her up and carried her up to the peach and ivory bedroom and simply held her until she stopped struggling and lay numbly in his arms. Then he started to undress her and as her breathing changed a slight, absent smile twisted his lips, causing her to get angry again and tell herself she hated him, but even in that angry, twisted way it was impossible to be unmoved by him. Impossible not to feel her breasts ache with desire when he lifted her up and kissed her nipples then tugged each one in turn with his teeth, and she arched her throat above his head, her hair falling down her back and her hands moving on his shoulders as she gasped with delight.

But it also became a contest as she returned his lovemaking step by step; somehow threaded through everything else she felt was an all-consuming desire to show him that she could give as good as she got—somehow she came alive with a chaotic storm of emotions that translated to a provocative sensuousness.

She used her body to tempt and delight him at the same time as she was unable to withstand the delight he was inflicting on her, on every slender limb, every curve and hollow and secret satiny place, until they were both bathed in sweat and the tension between them was unbearable and had only one release.

A release that left her crying with a tempestuous physical fulfilment but no peace in her heart. Nor in his apparently, because although he held her in his arms until the tears subsided he then got up, covered her, pulled on a pair of jeans and went to stand at the window with his back to her and a different kind of tension stamped into every line of his tall body.

Martha stared at him and swallowed several times, desperate to say something to end this nightmare, but finally he turned to her and said with no emotion, 'Get some sleep now—I've got a bit of work to do.' And he walked out, closing the door behind him.

Martha closed her eyes and pulled a pillow into her arms and wept more bitterly into it than she'd ever wept before.

It lasted over a fortnight, a state of armed neutrality where they saw little of each other, barely spoke when they did, where he made no attempt to touch her and slept in the other bedroom.

She went on as the kind of wife she'd become, taking care of his house, providing his meals, making sure his laundry was perfect and never forgetting his dry-cleaning, yet it seemed to her that she achieved all this in a state of suspended animation. Yvette was away again so she didn't have any work to help her take her mind off things, but she was grateful in one way because she doubted that she could fool Yvette.

And deep inside her there was always this feeling of helplessness, a feeling that there must be something she could do, but she knew that the only thing she could do was tell him she hadn't been with Ricky or anyone else. However, in her heart she knew it wasn't as simple as that; some intuition told her it was only the tip of the iceberg, and it became stronger as she relived the things he'd said and done time and time again. But her confusion grew at the same time. Why had he come home the way he had? Why should he be so irrationally jealous if the roots of this went back to Morag and not being able to forget her? Why be so determined to stay married to her if he did doubt her morals...? But every time she asked herself those questions the most likely answer seemed to be that, having entered this marriage, he was not about to let it be a failure.

Only it is—he must see that, she thought agonisingly. So why do I stay? Because I thought I'd found a home? Because I still can't help loving him? Because I'm a fool? Or has he even sapped all the resistance out of me as his father did to his mother?

It was two weeks to the day that she found a stray puppy—or rather it found her, followed her home and refused to be parted from her. It appeared to be mostly golden Labrador, had no collar, was a male and, she thought, about five months old. When he was still sitting outside the house half an hour after she'd got home, looking heartbroken, she let him in. From the way he fell on some food she offered, she guessed he'd been roaming around lost for a while.

A couple of days later he was still in residence despite every effort she'd made to find his owner. Nor was the owner of the house she lived in aware of its existence because he'd been in France since she'd found the dog.

Which was not calculated to improve his mood when he arrived home one cold, stormy afternoon, let himself in and was immediately confronted by an absolutely strange, savagely barking dog who obviously thought he was protecting the new, dearly loved and most important person in his life—Martha.

'What the hell . . . ?'

'*Sam*!' Martha grabbed the dog by his new collar. 'No, you mustn't. This is Simon; he lives here too.'

Sam subsided but was still growling softly, whereupon Simon raised his grey-green eyes to Martha and said with courteous yet barbed irony, 'Thank you. Is this some new plan to guard yourself from any ravishing designs I may have on you?'

She flushed and bit down on her own immediate desire to respond with equal irony. 'No. He's a stray; he followed me home one day.'

'Then you better get him to the RSPCA, Martha. I have no intention of being bitten and barked at in my own home.'

'Simon——' she took a breath '—could I keep him?'

His eyes raked over her but before he could say anything she went on hastily. 'Why don't you come down into the kitchen? I'll make you some tea or whatever. You look frozen—and he's more at home in the kitchen.'

There was an explosive moment when Simon murmured sardonically, 'By all means—if it means he's going to stop growling at me.'

Sam did, but reluctantly, and finally hopped into the basket Martha had made for him, but while he lay down with his head on his paws he didn't take his eyes off Simon for a moment.

Martha made tea as quickly as she could and as she was pouring it she said, 'I have rung the RSPCA to let them know he's here. And I advertised in the papers and I wrote out little notices and put them in some local shop windows but no one has come to claim him.'

'Go on.' Simon drank some tea then said irritably, 'For God's sake, can't you get him to stop staring at me?'

'Sam,' Martha said softly, and the dog leapt out of the basket, laid his head lovingly on her knee and wagged his tail with utter delight, while still keeping Simon well within sight. 'He's very affectionate,' she went on. 'He's been house-trained and——' She stopped abruptly and sighed.

'You've fallen for him,' Simon said.

'A bit,' she confessed. 'It gets lonely here sometimes,' she added barely audibly.

'What if he never takes to me?' he said after a moment.

'I'm sure he will so long as you—I mean...'

'Don't exhibit any animosity towards you?' he queried.

'Try to make friends with him,' she said evenly.

There was a tense little pause during which his gaze strayed over her arrogantly. 'And how do you propose I make friends with his mistress?' he said drily at last.

It was too much. 'If you don't know, don't bother!'

He smiled an unpleasant little smile at her and stood up. 'Very well. Sam,' he added, 'you may stay so long as we come to an agreement—no more foolishness.' And whether it was the tone of his voice or an air of command that was irresistible to canines she never knew, but in a few moments Sam was allowing himself to be patted and even followed Simon as he went upstairs, leaving Martha to stare unseeingly at her teacup.

Two days later Simon said to her at breakfast, 'We've been invited out to dinner tonight. Seven-thirty for eight. It's formal; I'll be wearing a dinner-suit. You haven't met the Carringtons but it's always silver service and butlers et cetera, they never invite less than thirty people, and you should dress accordingly. I'm sorry it's such short notice but I'd forgotten about it until my secretary reminded me. Perhaps Yvette could help you out in the matter of a dress—she'd know what was right.'

'Do you mean,' Martha said slowly, ignoring the implication that she herself mightn't know what was right, 'you expect us to go out as a couple tonight when we're not talking to each other?'

'Not only that but not sleeping with each other—yes, I do.' He lay back in his chair and watched the colour rise in her cheeks.

'You seem to have made that decision, Simon,' she pointed out.

He looked at her steadily, then said softly, 'Well, I'll tell you when I'm ready to reverse it, Martha.'

'Don't be too sure *I'll* be willing to reverse it, Simon.'

'That wasn't exactly what happened the last time,' he replied ironically.

She took a breath to steady herself but before she could say anything he went on thoughtfully, 'You know, so long as you stay, you're offering yourself up as a hostage of a kind.'

'Is that what you want me to do?' she whispered. 'Go? Even when you told me...when you said...' She couldn't go on.

'I can't chain you to my side despite what I said. Which is why I find it interesting that you of all people should stay to put up with this.'

'I told you once you didn't know me, Simon, but if it's any consolation I'm suffering from a certain amount of confusion, which is probably why I've stayed. But now you've made it plain——'

'I've made nothing plain,' he said harshly. 'Other than this: if you stay, we get back to being married in all senses of the word.' He stood up. 'I wonder if I'll see you tonight, Martha? I suppose only time will tell.' And he walked out.

For a couple of minutes Martha suffered a bout of extreme temper but even when it faded she was left with the curious conviction that she was being tested. She made the decision, still probably in the grip of some anger, that she wasn't going to be worsted in this test.

Accordingly she paid a visit to Yvette, who was back, and explained her mission. 'But I'll pay for this one,' she said with a faint smile.

Martha wondered if Yvette looked at her searchingly before she said slowly and as if her mind was elsewhere, 'The Carringtons? Very dressy...' Then her black eyes focused again. 'I know the very dress.'

It was black, a skin-tight, strapless dress, embroidered all over with looped ribbon and tiny rhine-

stones and it came with a full, long pewter satin coat
with a huge stand-up collar.

'Yes.' Yvette stood back critically. 'Certainly a *grande
dame* one, this one. You will slay the Carringtons,
Martha, but you've lost a little weight.'

'It's probably my dog,' Martha said with a wry smile.
'I have to walk him for miles otherwise he gets bored
and chews things.'

She went from Yvette to the beautician where she had
a facial and her nails done and thence to the hairdresser
and resolutely ignored the small voice that asked her why
she was doing this.

But just after she'd got dressed that evening, something happened that all but broke her heart and very
nearly did make her run away. When she heard Simon's
key in the lock she knew that she could not endure
another war of words with him and she emerged from
the peach bedroom as he was coming up the stairs.

'I'm sorry I'm late,' he said briefly. 'I'll only be a few
minutes; we've got to pick up another couple. You
look...' he paused '...stunning,' he said quietly, and
went into his bedroom.

But later, when she was standing beneath a crystal
chandelier divested of her coat and with an aperitif in
her hand, in what was undoubtedly a stately home, with
Maud Carrington chatting to her most amiably, she felt
Simon's presence beside her.

'Simon!' Maud said immediately. 'You two do make
the most smashing couple—have you come to claim your
wife? I don't blame you but I must warn you——' she
tapped him playfully on the wrist '—that you won't be
allowed to sit next to her at dinner.' And she drifted
away to mingle among her other guests.

'She's nice,' Martha said.

'Yes. What's wrong?'

She glanced up him, looking so tall and distinguished in his dinner-jacket, and felt her nerves tingle. 'Nothing. Am I doing something wrong?'

He took his time about answering as he examined the shining fall of her hair, the smooth curves of her throat and shoulders, the outlines of her figure beneath the black dress then back to the uncertainty in her blue eyes. 'No, but you look a little lost.'

Lost! her heart cried. What do you expect? But she said with some irony, 'Sorry, I'll try to liven up.'

'Martha——' He stopped as dinner was announced and his mouth hardened in irritation, she thought, and shivered inwardly because it could only be directed at her.

She was rescued in spite of herself, however, by being placed between two elderly gentlemen, one who payed her gallant courtly compliments throughout the meal and the other who knew Australia well. Simon, on the other hand, was between an unusually thin, intense opera singer and a busty woman with a boisterous laugh. But a couple of times, when Martha looked down the table at him, it was to find him watching her, although she couldn't read the expression in his eyes. And towards the end of the evening she thought suddenly, I shouldn't have done this; I shouldn't be doing *any* of this. I'll have to find the courage to go and the courage to tell him why...

There was no opportunity to do this in the car as they took home the elderly couple they'd picked up and who only lived two streets away.

But once inside the house on Onslow Square Martha nerved herself and instead of going straight to her bedroom went into the main drawing-room where she turned the lamps on and closed the curtains, and wondered if he would come.

He did after a few minutes, with a frown in his eyes. 'Where's the mutt?'

She smoothed the satin of her coat and tightened her hold on her composure. 'His owners turned up to collect him this evening. They were away and didn't know until today that he'd evaded the people looking after him, who never thought to ring the RSPCA.'

'So that's why you look as if your heart's breaking,' he said after a long, taut moment.

'Do I?' She raised her eyes to his at last. 'It is—but I suppose I'll get over Sam. Simon——'

'Are you about to tell me you won't get over me?' he queried. 'I can tell you all it will take to get us back on track—come to bed with me now, Martha. Let's put all this nonsense behind us.'

Her mouth quivered. 'How can you? How——?'

'We both know how I can,' he said sardonically. 'Do you want me to spell it out? All right, let's see . . .'

'No,' she whispered. 'Why are you taunting me into leaving you, Simon? Not that it matters—you've succeeded,' she stammered. 'I don't really know why things went so wrong; I was always prepared to accept that I might never take the same place as Morag in your heart, but not *this*. You may not want to hear it——' she twisted her hands together as he stood unmoving and watched the shadows that touched her pale, weary face '—and I did think you knew it anyway, but I love you,' she said simply. 'That's why I stayed, probably blindly and stupidly, probably because sometimes I'm much less sophisticated than you might have thought and the thought of a home—*any* kind of home—was better than none. But I finally got the message today—well, tonight. It's not enough for you, is it? Even if you're determined to go on because it's probably hard to admit to a failure like this and so soon.' She looked away at last.

He still said nothing, just stood tall and austere with a frown in his eyes but no other emotion.

Martha took a step to move past him, desperate to end this, but she was struck suddenly by another thought. 'By the way,' she said huskily, 'if you're worried about what I might want from you, there's nothing, and if you don't believe anything else about me you should believe that. All I *ever* wanted from you was to be loved.

'Perhaps you could have our solicitors get in touch with me before I go home. Oh, yes, and I wasn't with anyone the night you tried to ring me; I'd gone to the movies, that's all. It had been a difficult day. I lied to Yvette about Annabel because she wanted me to have dinner with her and Oswald and I just…knew I couldn't. For that matter,' she continued barely audibly, 'just as I've always known that Ricky was *never* for me. I don't know how to make you believe that; perhaps this is the only way—will you believe it when I've gone, Simon?'

There was a full minute's silence during which that clever gaze of his pinned her to the spot, seemed to see through her clothes and removed them from her body, seemed to be unmoved by the violet shadows beneath her eyes and—the unkindest thing of all—remind her vividly that her well-being was in his hands whether she liked it or not and that she was just about to made aware that apart from being taken to bed he wanted nothing more from her.

But he said abruptly at last, 'I know.'

'You *know*?' she whispered.

'I know now, but I have a devil riding me in some respects, Martha,' he said, and she shivered at the sudden bleakness in his eyes. He went on, 'I hope one day you can forgive me for what I've put you through one way and another but, you're right, this is not working; you're only completely wrong about the reason.'

Shock held her rigid.

He moved and came to stand right in front of her and went on with a strangely twisted smile, 'Don't look like that. It's better now than later, when you come to hate me.'

'Why?' It didn't sound like her voice, a ragged shaken sound, but she didn't care and went on, 'Because everything they *didn't* say about me is true? Because the difference between me and Morag is more than you can bear? Because I'm not wise and witty and all those things?'

A muscle moved in his jaw and the line of his mouth was hard again. 'No, that's not why. If anything you're too good, too decent, too lovely, too innocent, too...' He stopped and sighed. 'The problem is me. I can't love you the way you deserve to be loved. I thought I could but—look what happened the night I came home.'

Martha moved at last. 'Do you mean the suspicions you harboured?' she said uncertainly, because she had a sudden intuition that every word now spoken would take her into unchartered seas and she was desperately afraid of what she was going to hear.

'Yes, I mean exactly that,' he said grimly. 'I've always known you only had to lift your little finger and Ricky and his earldom around the corner would be yours; I was nearly insane with jealousy.'

She breathed unevenly. 'Simon, I may be a fool but I did wonder why, if you didn't feel anything for me, you would have cared where I was, why you came home anyway. I know I should have thought of that at the time, but, you see, there's been so much pressure on me——' She stopped.

'That's also been my doing, indirectly. But, you see, it's not love that's kept me bound to the memory of Morag, it's a terrible cynicism and lack of faith I can't break.'

Martha's lips parted and her eyes were stunned. 'I...I don't understand.'

'That's because I...' he paused and looked into her eyes bleakly '...took care that you wouldn't. I thought it was a way of protecting myself, but the truth of the matter is I ended up hating her; I was the one who called off the wedding a week before; I was the one who swore no woman would ever be able to put me in the position she did, but when she drove off in a rage and killed herself I was also the one suddenly bound to silence.'

'Simon,' Martha whispered dazedly.

'It doesn't make pleasant hearing, does it? I won't bore you with all the details——'

Martha said abruptly, '*Tell* me—I won't tell a living soul, I swear, but if there's *anything* between us,' she said anguishedly, 'don't shut me out any more. Don't you *realise* how much I love you? I know I may seem like a block of wood sometimes, and young and hungry for reassurance, lonely but——'

'Oh, God,' he said barely audibly and cupped her face gently, 'don't you realise I *love* you just the way you are but——?'

'N-no, no,' she stammered, 'you can't say that and expect me to believe it if you don't tell me why a few minutes ago you...said it wasn't going to work.'

He closed his eyes briefly. 'All right. Sit down.'

He waited until she sank into a settee, then shoved his hands into his pockets and paced around for a moment before he said, 'We were always enemies in a sense, Morag and I. We attracted each other and repelled each other at the same time. She was a spoilt, over-indulged

daughter of divorced parents with a mother who refused
her nothing and thought the sun shone out of her—
perhaps even tried to relive her own youth through her.
But Morag was also brilliant and fascinating, she fascinated and captivated most people, and it was only when
you ran into her determination always to have her own
way that the other side of her surfaced. I think that's
what both fascinated and repelled her about me. She
knew she couldn't always get her own way with me but
it didn't stop her trying. She knew that when I said no
I meant it but she couldn't always be sure when I would
say it and—looking back of course, these things are
always easier to see in hindsight—it generated the kind
of sparks between us that we both mistook for love. She
used to say to me after we were engaged, "You may
think you've got me where you want me, Simon, but I'll
still fight you—and you'll still marry me."'

He looked down at the floor then back into Martha's
eyes. 'And I used to think, Yes, I will, and then I'll really
have you where I want you...'

He stopped as Martha flinched, then grimaced as he
went on drily, 'I know—you see, her mother hadn't been
left very well off at all. Her father had not only divorced
her mother, but he fell on hard times and became
bankrupt so that all the things Morag had taken for
granted when she was growing up suddenly dried up
when she was about fifteen—the kind of things I could
give her again, the kind of standing in the community.'

'Are you saying she would have married you for your
money?'

'I'm saying it was a consideration,' he replied. 'Look,
I'm not trying to tell you Morag was...' he paused and
shrugged '...intrinsically wicked, for want of a better
word; perhaps what I'm trying to say is that despite the
attraction we brought out the worst in each other. For

example, when she made it plain she wanted a huge wedding with all the trimmings I went along with it, although privately I don't care much for those three-ring kind of circus weddings, and I paid for it. But when she told me she'd set her heart on having a year-long honeymoon——' He stopped abruptly as Martha made an agonised little sound, then went on, 'Doing all the things she'd longed to do, like seeing Mount Everest and travelling up the Amazon before there were no rainforests left to see et cetera, et cetera, I said no. That...' he paused '...was our final contest. But it dragged on for months, of course.'

Martha drew a shaken breath and whispered, 'I always had the feeling it started to go wrong from when I said all that about wishing I could take you away for a whole year, but I would never have——'

'You weren't to know,' he said roughly, then sighed. 'You may not believe this but I fought against being affected by something like that—only I didn't succeed too well. It seemed to open it all up again like a festering sore and, unbelievably, I started to get wary all over again; I started to think, Don't fall too much in love with this girl——' He stopped abruptly.

'So you called the wedding off?' Martha asked quietly after a long moment during which they stared into each other's eyes. 'But only a week...?' She stopped awkwardly.

'Yes,' he said with self-directed and bitter scorn. 'It sounds unbelievable, doesn't it? How could you get that close to marrying someone and only then realise that the attraction had perished somewhere along the line? But, you see, she'd been at great pains—perhaps I don't have to go into detail about that except to say that she was pretty experienced in that line—to keep it alive.'

'No,' Martha whispered, and coloured faintly.

'Why?' he asked in a different tone, watching the wash of pink cover her cheeks.

She bit her lip. 'I . . . it's just that I wanted to give you as good as I got that last night, something like that.'

'You did—the difference was you had no ulterior motive, but I'll tell about that in a while. What finally happened was—I think—that she sensed I was withdrawing quite some time before the last week and perhaps she got desperate and foolish, or perhaps she still believed I'd marry her—whatever; I've never really known. But when she came to me and told me she'd been to bed with another man and told me who it was, someone I knew well, I think she honestly believed that the thought of losing her would bring me round.'

Martha closed her eyes.

But Simon went on in that same even, emotionless voice, 'That was when I realised I could never live with her, that I despised and hated her, that the spell had finally broken. That was when——' he stopped and gritted his teeth briefly '—I looked at Morag and thought, Never again will *any* woman put me through this.'

'So you . . . so you . . .' Martha's voice shook.

'I told her the wedding was off. She . . . well, I've told you that bit; she drove off then and she died doing over a hundred miles an hour on an unsafe road.'

'And you don't think she was wicked?' Martha said uncertainly.

He sighed. 'I think some people can go either way. Some brilliant, highly-strung people. I think her mother was the worst possible influence she could have had.

Martha remembered that flash of vicious anger in Iris Wallace's eyes with a little tremor of fear. 'Did she know? I think she must have.'

'She guessed. Morag must have confided her doubts. She came to me and accused me of driving Morag to her death because I'd cancelled the wedding for no good reason, and that she'd make sure everyone knew. I told her the truth and I told her the only way she could guarantee that the memory of her daughter would not be dragged through the mire would be my silence—in exchange for hers. You might say we came to an agreement,' he finished with bitter irony.

'But you wouldn't have said anything anyway, would you?' Martha said.

'No, of course not, but when you're confronted by a mother who—well, least said about that the better. And in a sense I did feel guilty—I knew what Morag was like; I'd even played along with it to a certain extent, granting some of her desires, withholding others.' He gestured.

'And you've lived with that ever since?'

'Yes. That's the other reason I've had this black kind of cynicism in me, this...half-formed feeling that it might be better never to get too involved with anyone again. And that's what resurfaced too.'

Martha twisted her hands. 'She...her mother doesn't look poor now.'

'Iris? No, she isn't. She married again, an elderly millionaire, and is contriving to marry Morag's brother off, by the sound of it, to some girl who will live to regret the day—according to Yvette.'

A thought struck Martha. 'Did Yvette know?'

'No—well, I didn't tell her but I think she guessed— I don't think she really liked Morag and she always loathed Iris. I'm quite sure she only just restrained herself from telling me I was making an awful mistake at the time.'

'Grace liked her—Morag,' Martha whispered.

'I told you,' Simon said. 'She had her good side and her bad. She had me entranced for quite some time.'

Martha moved suddenly. 'Did you think of her as soon as you saw me? In Sydney? Another girl on the make sort of thing?'

'Yes.' He lifted an eyebrow. 'In a way, but you certainly had me confused at times, Martha.'

She grimaced. 'You didn't show it, but I did—sometimes I saw a darkness in you that I didn't think was wholly connected to me.'

'You were right.'

'And when I arrived in London?' she asked with a suddenly fearful expression.

'Do you know what struck me first?' he said slowly.

'Tell me.'

'That I'd never forgotten what it was like to kiss you, never forgotten the kind of sweet awakening in you before *you* remembered you didn't want me to think it was happening.'

'Then why——' she cleared her throat '—are you trying to tell me it can't work, Simon?'

'Because,' he said harshly, 'I'm afraid I'll kill it myself. Didn't you *tell* me tonight how well I was succeeding in doing just that.'

'So,' Martha said very quietly, 'are you saying you *can't* disassociate me from Morag—from the experience of her, I mean? That I have to pay for her sins even? I think, Simon, you've been kinder to her than you're being to me if that's the case. You're also forgetting there's been no man in my life other than you—does that mean *nothing*?'

'Martha,' he said intensely, 'I can *tell* myself these things, but it only took one instance of not being able to find you to bring it all back, to imagine *you* being unfaithful to me. It took much less than that, a few casual words,' he said bitterly, 'to decide you were growing into my heart and my life in a way that couldn't be allowed to happen——' He stopped abruptly.

'But,' she whispered, straining every nerve, taking every last gamble because she knew this was the most important moment of her life, 'isn't that why you came home? In case I'd bowed to the pressure and decided to leave?'

'Were you thinking of it?'

'I was thinking that you were regretting marrying me, but I was going to go on anyway, and when I had Sam...'

'Oh, God,' he said on a suddenly tortured breath, and sat down to gather her into his arms. 'Of course that's why I came home but——'

'Simon——' she broke free and touched his mouth gently '—that's all I want to hear. And there's no way you'll get rid of me now.'

'Doesn't the fact that I made you *say* you loved me, but wanted nothing from me before I could even start to tell you any of this, weigh with you, Martha? Doesn't the fact that I seduced you when I could no longer do without you and virtually forced you to marry me without being able to tell you how much I loved you weigh with you? Or the fact that I taunted you into deciding to leave me? It should,' he said grimly.

'The only thing that weighs with me is that I fell in love with you three years ago and it's never stopped,' she said simply. 'But you could tell me now,' she whispered, with sudden tears in her eyes, tears of reaction, relief. But she made herself go on, 'This little Aussie tart would——'

She got no further as he started to kiss her with a hunger that told its own tale. Then he took her coat off and simply stared at her before he pulled her on to his lap and said unsteadily, 'You're so beautiful, my little

Aussie tart. I'll never forget seeing you again at Yvette's cocktail party. I spent a hell of a night that night.' He cupped her shoulder then traced the outline of the black dress across the top of her breasts. 'And many more——' he laid his head back '—especially after I kissed you in the car and still you turned away from me. That actually made me so angry, I swore I'd get you out of my system once and for all.'

'I thought so,' she murmured. 'You were so furious when we met again on Mull.'

He grinned reminiscently. 'It didn't last long, though, did it?' Then he started to kiss her again with extreme urgency. 'I've spent some awful nights these past few weeks.'

'So have I,' she whispered.

'How can I ever make it up?'

'You don't have to. From the moment you said you loved me the way I *am*, it was like being healed,' she said softly.

'Do you know how jealous I was of Sam? How did he take being reclaimed?' he said irrelevantly some time later.

Her lips curved into a smile. 'He was overjoyed then bewildered and for just a moment he looked truly torn, but they have a little boy who adores him—that sealed it.'

'And you have a husband who adores you,' Simon said very quietly. 'Do you remember what I said to you once?'

'What?'

'God help any man who does fall in love with you...'

'Yes...'

'I've thought of that so often lately.' He stroked her cheek.

'It was a long time before I was any help. Simon.' She paused and looked up into his eyes. 'That last night...' She stopped and bit her lip.

'Ah, yes. My love,' he said gently, 'the way you made love to me...' He paused then said, 'The way *we* made love that night happened between two people in the grip of a similar emotion, but even though we were in a kind of anger with each other you were the only person in the world I wanted to be making love to and I think the same held good for you. That's what I meant when I said you had no ulterior motive. That's what made it so different from Morag. And only a bloody fool like me wouldn't have known it and told you so at the time. I've lived the past couple of weeks in a mixture of fear that I'd hurt you, and jealousy that I kept trying to tell myself was unfounded but I just couldn't seem to break myself out of it. I could see you drifting further and further away and, God help me, I couldn't help remembering that you'd always had a soft spot for Ricky—the only man you were ever comfortable with, in fact,' he said wryly and reminiscently.

'Simon,' she said softly, 'can I tell you something Annabel said to me once? She said it was always obvious that what was between us was way out of the boys' league. And it was—to me it was something so deep, powerful and mysterious that it had never let me go, never let me look at another man, and never would. I think,' she said tremulously, 'you'd better accept it now. What I would really like you to do is take me home to Mull, which would be a lovely place to—start a family.'

'Would you?' he said gently.

'Mmm... And catch fish better than you do.'

'That's debatable,' he replied gravely, but with a wicked little glint in his eye. 'I thought we were pretty evenly matched in that regard.'

'I told you a couple of times—you don't know me, Simon.'

He gathered her extremely close and said not quite steadily, 'But I'm beginning to at last. Martha, I don't know how you can have such faith in me after—everything.'

'Perhaps it has something to do with getting to the grand old age of twenty-two untouched by anyone else.'

His hands tightened on her. 'That makes me feel worse if anything.'

'Then——' she looked into his eyes with hers alight with love '—can I give you some advice? It's really only what you told me once: think of us in bed if any more doubts ever spring up.'

'I'm thinking of it right now.' He buried his face in her hair. 'I love you so much, Martha...'

Free Gift Offer

With a Free Gift proof-of-purchase
from any Harlequin® book, you can receive
a beautiful cubic zirconia pendant.

This stunning marquise-shaped stone is a genuine cubic
zirconia—accented by an 18" gold tone necklace.
(Approximate retail value $19.95)

Send for yours today...
compliments of ◆HARLEQUIN®

To receive your free gift, a cubic zirconia pendant, send us one original proof-of-purchase, photocopies not accepted, from the back of any Harlequin Romance®, Harlequin Presents®, Harlequin Temptation®, Harlequin Superromance®, Harlequin Intrigue®, Harlequin American Romance®, or Harlequin Historicals® title available in February, March or April at your favorite retail outlet, together with the Free Gift Certificate, plus a check or money order for $1.65 U.S./$2.15 CAN. (do not send cash) to cover postage and handling, payable to Harlequin Free Gift Offer. We will send you the specified gift. Allow 6 to 8 weeks for delivery. Offer good until April 30, 1997, or while quantities last. Offer valid in the U.S. and Canada only.

Free Gift Certificate

Name: _____

Address: _____

City: _____ State/Province: _____ Zip/Postal Code: _____

Mail this certificate, one proof-of-purchase and a check or money order for postage and handling to: HARLEQUIN FREE GIFT OFFER 1997. In the U.S.: 3010 Walden Avenue, P.O. Box 9071, Buffalo NY 14269-9057. In Canada: P.O. Box 604, Fort Erie, Ontario L2Z 5X3.

FREE GIFT OFFER
084-KEZ

ONE PROOF-OF-PURCHASE
To collect your fabulous FREE GIFT, a cubic zirconia pendant, you must include this original proof-of-purchase for each gift with the properly completed Free Gift Certificate.

084-KEZ

Heartbreak RANCH

Four generations of independent women...
Four heartwarming, romantic stories of the West...
Four incredible authors...

Fern Michaels
Jill Marie Landis
Dorsey Kelley
Chelley Kitzmiller

Saddle up with Heartbreak Ranch, an outstanding
Western collection that will take you on a whirlwind
trip through four generations and the exciting,
romantic adventures of four strong women who
have inherited the ranch from Bella Duprey,
famed Barbary Coast madam.

Available in March,
wherever Harlequin books are sold.

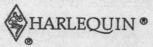

HARLEQUIN ®

HTBK

You're About to Become a *Privileged Woman*

Reap the rewards of fabulous free gifts and benefits with proofs-of-purchase from Harlequin and Silhouette books

Pages & Privileges™

It's our way of thanking you for buying our books at your favorite retail stores.

PROOF OF PURCHASE
HP-PP23
Offer expires March 31, 1997

Harlequin and Silhouette—
the most privileged readers in the world!

For more information about Harlequin and Silhouette's PAGES & PRIVILEGES program call the Pages & Privileges Benefits Desk: 1-503-794-2499

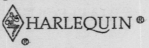
HARLEQUIN ®

HP-PP23